MW00615769

To: Arlene

Shadows of Time

Valerie Massey Goree

" Let us then approach
God's throne of grace
with confidence... "
       Hebrews 4:16

Goree

Copyright © 2022 by Valerie Goree
Published by Forget Me Not Romances,
an imprint of Winged Publications

Editor: Cynthia Hickey
Book Design by Forget Me Not
Romances

All rights reserved. No part of this
publication may be reproduced, stored in a
retrieval system, or transmitted in any form or
by any means—electronic, mechanical,
photocopying, recording, or otherwise—
without the prior written permission of the
publisher. The only exception is brief
quotations in printed reviews. Piracy is illegal.
Thank you for respecting the hard work of this
author.

TRIGGERS:

General genetic manipulation
Genetic research pre- and post-WWII in
Germany
References to the atrocities of the
Holocaust

Scriptures used are from the NIV
Zondervan, 1985

ISBN: 978-1-956654-71-4

Dedication

Thank you to my children from the bottom of my heart for helping me navigate this past traumatic year and a half. The illness and passing of their father and my beloved husband, Glenn. Selling up and moving from Washington State back to Texas. Settling in my new home. I would not have survived without your love and support.

Thank you, Father God for your constant guiding hand over my life.

Acclaim for Valerie Goree's Books

Deceive Me Once

"This book held my interest from the first page. I loved the main character with her faults and strengths. The ending was gripping and totally satisfying."

*Amazon Reader Review

Colors of Deceit

"This is an intriguing, suspenseful and page turning book that will keep you guessing until the end."

*Amazon Reader Review

Weep in the Night

"Very well written and a page turner, this story kept me up late at night reading just a little bit more..."

*Amazon Reader Review

Day of Reckoning

"This Christian romantic suspense novel drew me in and kept me hooked."

*Amazon Reader Review

Justice at Dawn

"It was a definite page turner, on the edge of your seat throughout the book."

*Amazon Reader Review

Forever Under Blue Skies

"*Forever Under Blue Skies* made me want to visit Australia. The two mysteries woven into the story kept me turning the pages and the proposal was so romantic, I had to read it twice."

*Amazon Reader Review

"…for we were born only yesterday and know nothing,
and our days on earth are but a shadow."
Job 8:9 (NIV)

Chapter 1

The choppy waters of Puget Sound slapped against the side of the ferry as Anna Knight scanned Seattle's iconic skyline. Although the morning sunlight glistened off the whitecaps, the brisk sea air gave her goosebumps. Rubbing her bare arms, she climbed into her vehicle. Anna seldom visited the city and was not looking forward to meeting with her mother's attorney for the reading of the will. As an only child with no relatives, she expected to receive the majority of the estate. However, Claire Taylor was anything but predictable. Following her mother's sudden death, Anna discovered that besides the family home on Bainbridge Island, she also owned a condo in one of Seattle's prestigious downtown neighborhoods. The lawyer might reveal more surprises.

While Anna drove off the ferry and through the city to Maureen Webb's office, anxious rumblings filled her stomach. Reviewing Mother's will was Anna's final official duty. After the meeting, maybe she could grieve.

1

Anna parked along the curb, entered the first-floor office, and introduced herself to the dainty receptionist who wore a well-fitting aqua dress.

"Good morning, Ms. Knight." She set down her coffee mug. "Would you care for a latte? Cappuccino?"

Although the pleasant, nutty aroma of quality coffee wafted through the small room, Anna declined. She'd already consumed her limited caffeine quota for the day.

Clutching her purse, Anna followed the young lady to a corner office. Her three-inch heels click-clicked on the marble floor.

Maureen Webb sat behind a large, steel and glass desk. The attorney, dressed in a lemon-yellow suit, stood and tucked ink-black strands of hair behind her ear. Numerous gold bracelets jingled on her wrist as she extended her hand which displayed crimson nails that clashed with her deep olive skin.

Anna shook hands, then sat, regretting her appearance. Hair twisted in a knot on top of her head, no doubt with tendrils blown loose by the wind. Blue jeans, T-shirt, sandals. After all, she wasn't teaching at her art institute this summer and hadn't even thought to dress up for the visit.

"Ms. Knight, I know this must be stressful for you." The lawyer donned a pair of ebony-rimmed glasses. "First, I need two forms of picture identification, please."

Passport and driver's license placed on the desk, Anna leaned back in the plush chair and tried to relax by slowing her breathing.

Ms. Webb studied the passport. "Annika Louis Knight. Is Knight your married name?"

"No. I have my father's last name. Mother kept her maiden name."

"I see." She set aside the items then opened a folder. "I'll give you a copy of the will before you leave—"

"Wait. How come you asked if I was married? Didn't Mother discuss such matters with you?" Claire might have been aloof with Anna, but surely, she'd be open with her lawyer.

"We met two months ago. She only came to my office twice."

Knots tightened in Anna's stomach. "Two months. Right after she got sick." Mother's sudden illness and rapid decline now took on an extra layer of unease. "I suppose you didn't have time to socialize."

"No. Your mother knew exactly what she wanted." Ms. Webb held up a document. "Are you ready?"

As I'll ever be. Anna nodded and crossed her legs. "Don't bother to read all the legalize. Just get to the heart of the matter."

"Right. Claire Taylor asked me to be the executor." She paused. "Does that surprise you?"

"No. Mother never credited me with any business sense. And actually, I'm relieved."

"She stipulated payment of taxes and settling her debts, listed several bequests. All her physical property is yours, but the rest of her assets are divided equally between you and the Nachwelt Foundation."

Anna frowned. A charity? Mother never expressed any interest in helping other people, let alone leaving money to an organization. "I know Nachwelt is German for posterity, but I've never heard of this foundation."

"You speak German?"

"Yes."

"I'm not at liberty to divulge any more details, as per Ms. Taylor's directions."

"Okay, I suppose it really doesn't matter." Anna cleared her throat. "Other than the house on Bainbridge Island, her condo here in town, and her vehicle, what else did she own? She didn't share her business dealings with me, nor her day-to-day life."

Ms. Webb straightened in her leather chair, removed her glasses and said, "You didn't know much about your mother, did you? Your share of her assets is in excess of forty-five million."

Anna's eyebrows shot up. "Dollars?" She gulped and stood, her knees ready to buckle.

"Yes. She stipulated that you not investigate the foundation."

"I have no plans to investigate anything or anyone. I have to get out of here." Anna slung her purse strap over her shoulder. She struggled to breathe as the room seemed to shrink. *Not now.* "You're right. I didn't know my mom at all. How did she accumulate that much wealth?" Backstepping toward the door, she shook her head. "Please mail me a copy of the will." Anna stormed out of the office, her adrenaline-fueled blood on fire.

Chapter 2

By the time Anna reached the house on Bainbridge Island, she'd calmed down enough to realize she was a millionaire, but had no idea what to do next. Except call her best friend. First, she set a mug of water in the microwave to heat then checked the wall clock above the sink. Just after noon. Lexie was teaching this summer, but should be on break.

She answered right away. "Hey, Anna. How'd it go? You all right?"

"Sort of. I'll tell you everything when we meet tomorrow." Maybe not everything until she'd found answers to alleviate her doubts.

"Your voice is a bit shaky."

"I...I almost lost it in her office, but the ferry ride gave me time to go through my calming routine."

"Why don't you come by the studio so I can give you a hug?"

"Thanks, but no. I have so much to think about, and I need a good lawyer."

"That bad, eh? I'll continue to pray for you, sweet ladybug. As to legal advice, I highly recommend the attorney my mother-in-law used. He's here in Port Townsend."

Anna retrieved the mug and added an orange and ginger teabag, one item in her mother's pantry she appreciated. "Text me his contact info, please."

"Will do. Got to eat a quick lunch before my next group arrives. Wish you were with us this session. See ya."

Sipping the hot gingery brew, Anna strolled through the house to the office. Although she'd lived here from birth until she'd left for university—her ninety-day stint in Juvie aside—she'd never set foot in her mother's sanctum until the day after her death, four weeks ago.

Anna stopped in the doorway and drew in a deep breath. Hints of Mom's floral but subtle perfume lingered in the room. She must have spent a lot of time in there for the scent to cling to the carpet, drapes, and the upholstered desk chair. Blinking back a tear of regret, Anna entered and set her cup on a coaster on the desk. She could have called more often. Stopped by for a visit. Ignored her mother's standoffish attitude and insisted on establishing adult connections. Afterall, she'd never had another run-in with the law, and she had her anxiety disorder well under control. Two issues Mother had frequently used to berate Anna.

She shook her head. Now was not the time to dwell on missed opportunities. After the reading of the will, Anna had a compelling reason to search through the file cabinets and drawers. How had Mother accumulated her wealth, and what was the Nachwelt Foundation? Although Anna had previously made a preliminary rifle through papers on the desk and in the drawers where she'd found the deed to the condo, she now probed every nook and cranny where documents might be stored or hidden.

Hours later, she was no closer to finding answers than she'd been at the start. Mother kept meticulous records from her local bank, tabulated utility costs, neatly filed correspondence from her place of business, FARA—Frank Ahn Research Associates, which had headquarters in Seattle. Anna had never visited, but would make a point of clearing out that office soon. Sitting on the floor surrounded by folders and papers, she pursed her lips. When her friends from junior high school had gone with a parent for 'take you daughter to work' day, Claire always refused the opportunity. "I work in the scientific world, child. My days are filled with meetings and phone calls. Reading reports. Nothing for you to see or do. However, when you show an interest in my field of expertise, I'll consider taking you."

That day never came. Although Anna graduated from the University of Washington with a double major in biology and chemistry, by then she had no interest in going to work with Mom. In fact, she regretted her choice of study, subjects chosen to please her mother, and since Anna didn't receive straight *As*, Mom wasn't impressed. Anna realized she was not intelligent enough in her mother's estimation and nothing she did would ever earn her love. All perceptions which contributed to Anna's escalating symptoms of an anxiety disorder and eventual diagnosis and treatment during her sophomore year.

However, since Mother continued to pay tuition, Anna followed her passion and graduated top of her class with a master's degree in art. Using money left to her by her father, she and Lexie established the Hugh Knight Institute of Art located in Port Townsend, named in his honor, of course. In spite of periodic financial woes, the past three years had been the happiest of her life.

Anna stood and set her hands on her hips. The amount of the legacy sat heavy on her heart. What kind of research did her mom conduct that garnered her millions? But with her inheritance, Anna could buy the whole building where they now rented a few rooms for the institute. Offer scholarships, expand the curriculum, hire more staff. "Thanks, Mom." She smirked, considering the irony. Her skills as a graffiti artist had landed her in Juvie at age eleven. When she returned home, Mother had even forbidden her the use of a set of watercolors.

Empty mug in hand, Anna retreated to the kitchen and heated a frozen pizza. Bonnie Wakefield, the part-time housekeeper, had agreed to come in twice a week, Tuesdays and Fridays, to dust and vacuum, and to keep a few quick meals stocked in the freezer. Anna nabbed a notepad and pen from the junk drawer, and as she ate, she made an inventory of items she'd take from the house. A comfortable armchair her dad had loved. His chess set, carved marble pieces in charcoal and white. No doubt she'd sell the mansion and most of the contents. Mother had exquisite taste in furnishings, décor, clothes, and jewelry, but all were too elegant for Anna's simple lifestyle. Years ago, she'd taken possessions from her own bedroom and now could think of little else she wanted except photographs.

Framed pictures jostled for space on the oak mantel above the enormous fireplace. Anna recognized few who weren't family. She stacked the selected photos on one end, left a note for Bonnie stating she took them, then stared at the large painting displayed on the brick chimney. A flower garden in vibrant colors painted by German artist, Emil Nolde.

An idea brewed in her mind. Other than visiting Mother recently when she was ill, Anna hadn't been in the house for a long time and had almost forgotten the paintings displayed in almost every room. Of course, some were prints, but many were originals, like the Nolde. Anna could exhibit the masterpieces in the institute and use them for inspiration and instruction for her student. She ran from room to room, documenting the art works she wanted. Two portraits by Franz Xavier Winterhouse, a still-life by Paul Cézanne, Herman Hesse landscapes, a beach scene by Monet, and three expressionist pictures by August Macke.

For the first time all day, Anna smiled. At last, she could incorporate some of Mother's treasures into her life. She entered the den intent on removing the photographs from the mantel. The one on top was of her father sitting in his favorite chair. Anna clasped it to her chest, hobbled to the chair, and collapsed. Tears ran freely down her cheeks as sobs racked her body. She wasn't sure if the tears were for her dad, her mom, or herself, but minutes later, she snatched a tissue from the side table, wiped her eyes, and sucked in a breath.

Surprised Mother had kept Papa's chair all these years, Anna drew up her legs and snuggled against the gray, corded fabric. She stared at his picture and traced the outline of his oval face. He'd died a month after her sixth birthday, but she could still recall his gentle touch, his soft voice. His words, "Now, now, my little Annika. Don't fret. Your mother is busy. I'll read to you whenever you want." And he had. Every night before bed, and any other time she found him sitting alone.

Studying the photo with adult eyes, Anna noticed how old he seemed. He'd always been old to her, but didn't all little kids think every adult was ancient? She'd inherited his unusual gray eyes with amber flecks surrounding the pupils and Mother's blonde hair, including the white streak on the left side, but often wished she had his dark brown curls.

She looked closely at the photo one last time and spied a slim chain around his neck. Another buried memory surfaced. Seated on his lap after he'd read to her, she stroked his bearded chin, his neck, and found the chain. She pulled it out and asked why he wore a crucifix—a friend from school wore one and explained its significance to Anna.

Papa never raised his voice to her, but on that occasion his deep tone scared her. "Don't do that again, little Annika. Forget what you've seen, and never tell Mother. She keeps many secrets from you, so let this be our little secret." Then his tone softened. "I'm sorry for what we did."

Since Papa died soon after that episode, Anna never had the opportunity to ask him what he apologized for or about Mother's secrets and didn't mention the incident to her. As Anna grew older, she knew why. Mother was an atheist. Anything to do with religion was scorned and criticized. How could any intelligent person believe such nonsense? No wonder Papa hid his crucifix.

Maybe because Anna didn't have a warm, loving relationship with her mother, she didn't uphold her beliefs. When she met Lexie Vaughn in art school, Anna was open to hearing about God and the Bible.

Lexie was the sincerest person she'd ever met. Over a two-year period, her friend studied with her, made her question what she remembered from her mother's indoctrination, but never preached nor demeaned. Anna had been on the verge of accepting Jesus as her Savior several times, but she still hesitated, doubting she was worthy of such love and forgiveness. Prior to her diagnosis, she'd used illicit drugs to help navigate through life, the side effects of many exacerbated her symptoms. Her past indiscretions where never far from her conscious mind, enveloping her in self-loathing.

Heaving a sigh, she stood and collected the stack of photos from the mantel. She placed the frames side-by-side on the coffee table and examined the pictures. Except for a few forehead wrinkles, Mother never seemed to age. The only aspect that changed was her coiffure and the color of her hair. Blonde pageboy to silver chignon.

Anna picked up the frames, collected her purse from the kitchen, and headed to the front door. She ran a finger over her smooth forehead. "Mother, I hope I've inherited more than your left-handedness and blonde hair."

Chapter 3

Who knew cyber tricks perfected during his misspent youth would result in such a lucrative career? Cullen Kincaid patted his shirt pocket where his latest payment resided. A check large enough to cover his mortgage for at least five months. He closed the door to Attorney Jerome Jennings's office and sauntered down the stairs to the sidewalk.

His latest job entailed locating assets a man had hidden from his soon-to-be ex-wife. Success. Her divorce settlement would now keep her and their three young children in modest comfort. As a freelance operative utilizing every legal option available, Cullen often worked for lawyers. His favorite gigs were when his skills resulted in financial betterment for people who suffered when their so-called loved ones twisted the laws in their favor.

As was his custom after every tech-assisted win, he snapped the braided black elastic band he wore with his watch. The image of Reed Anderson, his high school pal, seized his mind and his satisfaction faded. The prank Cullen had played on him when they were hot-headed teens had ultimately led to his friend's death. Squaring his shoulders, Cullen huffed out a sigh.

Working as designed, the black band emphasized his determination to atone for his past.

Instead of driving to the bank, Cullen strode down the sidewalk. The speed with which people moved out of his way prompted him to soften his expression. Friends often told him his size, dark hair, dark eyes, and square jaw accompanied by a scowl were enough to scare away the toughest thug.

After depositing his check, Cullen checked his watch. Only four thirty. He had plenty of time to go home and review his lesson for the midweek Bible study, eat supper, then shower and change.

His unpretentious little house occupied a corner lot on the bluff overlooking Port Townsend's waterfront. He gathered his study materials and sat in a rocking chair on the porch. Bits of gravel crunched with each movement of the chair. Time to sweep the area, but Cullen had been too busy to take care of outside chores.

Tom Vaughn, his teaching partner, had concluded his lessons on prayer, and Cullen had agreed to tackle the subject of forgiveness. He turned to his key Scripture, Ephesians 1:7–8, and read the verses. "In him we have redemption through his blood, the forgiveness of sins, in accordance with the riches of God's grace that he lavished on us with all wisdom and understanding."

Why, oh, why, had he taken on this topic? No matter how many verses on forgiveness he read, Cullen had never reached the point where he could forgive himself for Reed's death.

He closed his Bible and dropped to his knees. "Help me, Father God. I have no business teaching anyone about forgiveness when I can't accept Your grace."

~

A small group of people of all ages gathered in the courtyard of Vaughn's Vittles, Tom's restaurant. On Wednesday evenings, he reserved the area for the Bible study. Cullen helped arrange chairs in a semi-circle, then returned to his seat where he'd propped his guitar case earlier. Although the sun wouldn't set for a couple of hours, Tom had turned on the strings of little twinkling lights surrounding the courtyard. That, and the fragrant and colorful flowers in large pots created a peaceful ambiance.

Cullen strummed harmonious chords as people sat and conversed. Out of the corner of his eye, he noticed Lexie, Tom's wife, enter the courtyard with a stranger. The blonde clutched the strap of her purse as if it were her lifeline. When Lexie introduced her to friends, she brandished a smile that immediately slid from her lips. Although there were two empty chairs beside him where Cullen hoped Lexie would settle, she chose seats opposite his. Not to worry. He could now keep an eye on her guest as he played. The woman set her purse on her lap, but her knee bounced so rapidly, she clutched the bag to her chest. Her gaze frequently flew to the gate that led to the path around back. She acted as if she didn't want to be here. He wouldn't be surprised if she bolted any second.

But she stayed through the singing, the prayers, and his lesson. He wasn't sure how he'd managed to lead the discussion for thirty minutes without choking. The Holy Spirit must have been on double-duty as his helper.

Tom voiced the closing prayer, and Cullen noticed the guest stand and head for the gate, followed by

Lexie. He hurried after them. "Lexie, who's your friend?" He had to intervene before she disappeared.

The blonde attempted to open the latch, but Lexie set her arm around her shoulders and whispered, "Please stay."

"All right. Only a few minutes." Her soft voice held a note of melancholy that stabbed at Cullen's heart.

"Hi. I'm Cullen Kincaid." He extended his hand.

"This is my business partner, Anna Knight." Lexie stood between the gate and her friend.

Cullen took Anna's small hand in his and stared into her face. In spite of the warm evening, her hand was cold, as were her unusual gray eyes that had amber flecks around the pupils. He sensed sadness and apprehension. Caused by attending a Bible study, or was she in some kind of trouble?

"It's a pleasure to finally meet you. Lexie has—" Lexie's subtle kick at his shin halted his words.

"Anna had a taxing day. I've invited her many times and finally persuaded her to come tonight, but I'd rather we don't smother her with questions on her first visit." The tilt of Lexie's head and her raised eyebrows warned Cullen to ease up.

He stepped back in acknowledgement, aware of how his size and deep, authoritative voice intimidated people. "I understand. Come again, Anna." Dipping his head, he walked away, but seconds later, he turned in time to see Anna turn, too. Their gazes locked for a few seconds and something happened in his chest. Now he understood when people said their hearts skipped a beat.

The lights emphasized Anna's golden hair, high cheek bones, and vulnerable eyes. She raised her hand in a brief wave, so brief he wasn't sure if she'd made the movement, but he returned the salute anyway.

Seated with his guitar on his lap, Cullen shook his head. His day had brought him a good payment for a worthy deed along with a stark reminder of his friend Reed and meeting a woman with sad gray eyes. The flutter in his heart at the mere thought of Anna signaled maybe he wasn't prepared for the outcome of their encounter.

Chapter 4

While sitting in the attorney's reception room, Anna had plenty of time to reread her mother's will. It still made little sense to her. Lexie had recommended Jerome Jennings, but Anna had to wait until Monday for an appointment. In the meantime, she'd returned to the Bainbridge Island house and made another search for anything that would answer her questions. She found nothing helpful and decided to give up working on her own. Maybe Mr. Jennings could provide some insight.

Phil Green, the receptionist, glanced up as a portly man in a tan suit strode into the room and held out his hand. "Sorry to keep you waiting, young lady. I'm Jerome. Come on in." His Texan accent surprised her.

Anna's hand disappeared into his paw as he drew her toward his office. He opened the door with a flourish.

"Now, have a seat, missy, and tell me what's eatin' ya."

He wasn't exceptionally tall, but his girth and boisterous personality made him seem gigantic. Sinking into his desk chair, he clasped his hands over his paunch and rocked. His white bowtie and orange shirt added a flair to his plain suit.

She settled into a leather armchair. "I told Mr. Green—"

"Yes, yes, I know. But I want to hear your story in your own words."

She crossed then uncrossed her legs. Although she knew exactly what she wanted to say, the words gummed up in her throat. To postpone the telling a bit longer, she glanced at a vase of lavender on the desk. Without thinking, she crushed the blooms on one stalk between her thumb and forefinger. The pleasant aroma had a calming effect.

Mr. Jennings ignored her action, stopped rocking, and set his elbows on the desk. "Now, child. It's always difficult to discuss the loss of a parent. But I can't help until I understand your needs."

"I want to know how Mother made her money and who or what is the Nachwelt Foundation?"

"Now, that's better. Specifics. I can deal with specifics. You have a copy of her will?"

"Yes." Anna handed it over, and while Mr. Jennings read it, she reiterated her surprise at the contents.

He leaned back so far, Anna thought Mr. Jennings would topple out of his chair. But he straightened and set the document on his desk. "An uncomplicated will, in my estimation. All seems in order, but I can understand why you're concerned. Your mother's assets were extensive, to say the least. Are you considering contesting the will?"

"No. I had no idea she'd accumulated that much wealth. I don't care if I only get half."

"Then how do you think I can help?"

"Well, Mr. Jennings, you came highly

recommended, and I was told—"

"Call me Jerome, darlin', and I hope you don't mind the endearment. I mean nothin' by it, 'ceptin', you're so young and all."

"Uh, no." To tell the truth, Anna hadn't even noticed. The words seemed to spill from his effervescent personality. "I read the part where my mother stated she didn't want me to investigate the foundation, but I couldn't find any provision that such an action would nullify her will."

"You're right. Maybe she thought you would comply with her wishes. Did you always do as she stipulated?"

Anna burst out laughing, then sobered. "No. The exact opposite."

Rocking again, Jerome clasped his hands and pursed his full lips. "Interesting. Almost as if she wants you to investigate."

Except for a distant car horn, silence reigned in the office. Anna stared at her feet, then at the attorney. Could he be right? "I have so many questions, I can't think straight."

"Do you want to hear my suggestions?"

She nodded.

"There's no hurry for you to do anything with your inheritance. Leave all as is until you get your answers. But at some point, you must hire an accountant or financial adviser, an estate planning attorney, a tax attorney. Until you've done that, don't tell people of your good fortune."

"I've only told my best friend."

"Good. As far as your queries go, your mother's source of wealth might be connected to the Nachwelt

Foundation. Either way, I know someone who should be able to delve into that world. Are you sure you want to investigate?"

"Yes." Anna never expected a windfall from her mother and before she became used to the idea of being a multi-millionaire, she had to discover the truth. Especially since it seemed Mother expected her to probe.

"Right." Jerome hollered, "Phil."

The receptionist opened the door and peeked in.

"Please contact Cullen Kincaid." Jerome sat back and grinned as Phil left the office.

Kincaid? Anna frowned. The man who led the Bible study.

The phone rang, and Jerome held it to his ear. "Thanks, Phil." He paused. "Kincaid, I have a job for you." A few uh-huhs, then he looked at her. "Can you meet him tomorrow at noon?"

With nothing on her calendar but a lunch date with Lexie on Thursday, Anna shrugged. She did want answers. "Noon will be fine."

"Great." A couple of second later, Jerome hung up. "He suggested Vaughn's Vittles. You can't miss him. He'll be the only man in the place who looks like a professional wrestler, over six feet tall and, well, muscular. Have your heard of such a restaurant?"

Nodding as she stood, Anna clung to her purse. "Thanks, Jerome." She left the office in a daze. Cullen's lesson last Wednesday evening had brought her to the verge of accepting that God's grace was meant for her, too. If the man couldn't find answers about her mother, maybe he could banish the last vestige of doubt around her soul.

SHADOWS OF TIME

Chapter 5

More concerned with Kincaid's sleuthing skills than her appearance, Anna didn't bother to change out of her work clothes—paint-splattered blue jeans and gray T-shirt. No matter what size smock she wore, the acrylic paint found its way around the edges. Her latest project took her out of her comfort zone. An abstract rendition of an ocean scene, and, in spite of scrubbing her hands, telltale signs of the blues and grays she'd recently used dotted her skin.

Anna needn't have worried. Kincaid sat at a table in the courtyard. He stood as she approached, hands on his blue-jean-clad hips, and his faded black T-shirt appeared ready for the rag pile. He appeared much taller in daylight and his grin softened the harsh lines of his jaw.

"Anna, good to see you again. I'd invite you to join me but I'm waiting for a client."

The attorney hadn't mentioned her name. "Jerome sent me."

"Aha. Not a chance meeting." He towered over her. "Please sit, and let's order before we discuss business." Cullen beckoned a waiter who set menus on the table beside a black leather portfolio.

Savory aromas emanated from plates of steak and salmon at the next table. But the idea of eating curdled Anna's stomach. "If you don't mind, I'll just have lemonade. Thank you for coming, Mr. Kincaid."

"Call me Cullen. I don't like cooking, so I eat out as often as possible." He looked at the waiter and said, "The veggie burger, please, and substitute a baked potato for the fries. No butter or sour cream. And a glass of water."

What an enigma. A man three times her size who could probably pick her up as easily as she did a gallon of milk ordered a vegetarian meal. He was also a guitar-playing Bible teacher and computer expert. Well, if he found answers to her dilemma, he could have any number of unusual traits and she wouldn't care.

After the waiter delivered their order, Kincaid bowed his head. "Father, God, thank You for our blessings. Please give me the wisdom to know how to help Anna. Amen." He sliced his burger in half. "Hope you don't mind me praying."

She shook her head. Who was she to object? "Shall I tell you what I need?"

"Yes. I'll take notes while I eat." He opened the portfolio and nabbed a pen.

"You use paper and pencil?"

"Yup. Information entered into any form of technology can always be retrieved. By the good guys or the bad. But paper can be destroyed. I don't even use online banking. I prefer to conduct all my transactions in person, in a brick-and-mortar location. Fire away." He fisted half the burger in his left hand and took a bite.

Anna explained the problems her mother's will presented. Cullen took notes and asked a couple of clarifying questions. By the time he finished his meal, she had revealed all she knew and what she wanted. She'd managed the whole interchange with composure.

He wiped his mouth and pushed aside his empty plate. "All sounds doable. First, have you done any research into the foundation?"

"No, but Nachwelt is German for posterity."

"How—?"

"My mother spoke German, and to impress her, I studied the language all through high school." Anna cradled the glass of lemonade in her hands and tilted her head. "Look, I was shocked by Mother's sudden illness and death, and then learning the contents of her will overwhelmed me to such an extent I've been unable to think straight."

"I understand. The 'Posterity' Foundation. Does that ring any bells?"

"It means nothing to me."

"But it's a beginning." Cullen paid the bill the waiter presented, then reviewed his notes. "What do you know about your mother's place of employment, Frank Ahn Research Associates?"

"FARA? Not much. She once told me she attended lots of meetings and read reports. Since her degrees are all in the sciences, I imagine she did her share of research, too. I've never even been to her office. I will soon, though, to collect her personal items."

"Good. I'll accompany you."

"Okay. Why?" Anna immediately regretted her question. Having a tough-looking guy with her would boost her confidence to no end.

"I can snoop while you pack." Frowning, he looked at her. "When did Claire pass away?"

"A month, no five weeks ago."

"You might not be able to see her office. They've probably replaced her by now."

Anna rolled her eyes. "What did I tell you? My thoughts are a jumbled mess."

"Did you ever check her business online? Weren't you curious?"

A shower of sadness sprinkled over Anna, and she slumped in the chair. Whatever curiosity she had ceased when Mother spurned her questions time and again, always hinting that Anna wasn't smart enough to comprehend the work she did. "I was curious, but a person can only take so much rejection. And, to tell the truth, I really didn't care what she did."

"I'm sorry. I'll only pry further if necessary." Cullen withdrew a sheet of paper from his portfolio. "This is my standard contract. Although Jerome is employing me, I want you to be aware of the scope of my skills. I can't promise I'll always get the desired results, but I'll certainly use all my expertise to reach a satisfactory conclusion."

Anna skimmed the document. If it was good enough for Jerome, it was peachy for her. "Is this my copy?"

"Yup. One more caveat—I have two other cases I'm working on. They are long term and don't require my constant involvement. Okay?"

Nodding, she folded the contract and slipped it into her purse.

"Do you want to go to Seattle today?" He zipped up his portfolio and tucked it under one arm.

She mentally calculated the time involved. "No. It's late, and I want to stop by her condo in the city. Before you ask, I haven't been there either. I only found out about it after she died."

"Tomorrow, then, but I have to be back by seven to teach the Wednesday Bible class. Good idea to search the condo. Since you didn't know about it, maybe your mother has information there that will answer your questions."

"I never thought of that." She chuckled. "That's why you earn the big bucks. However, I did search her home office." Anna was disappointed when Cullen didn't react to her stab at humor. "We can take an early ferry from Bainbridge. Where should I pick you up?"

Cullen beamed a bright grin at her and stood. "Since I'll be adding the trip to my expense account, I'll drive. Motorbike or Jeep?"

"Motorbike?" Sitting behind him, in close proximity. "No, thanks."

"Jeep it is, then. Bear in mind, my vehicle is old but reliable." He handed her a business card. "Here's my contact information. Text me your address. What time?"

"Seven. We can visit the condo first, then be at the office by ten."

"I need access to your mother's computer and cell phone. Can you give them to me tomorrow?"

"She didn't have a desktop computer, and the housekeeper said Mother always took her laptop with her. I couldn't find her phone. Maybe she left the items at the condo or in her FARA office."

"Good. See you in the morning." He doffed an imaginary hat and exited the courtyard via the gate.

Although Anna was sure she could handle the office visit and a search of the condo by herself, having Cullen accompany her made her feel safe, protected.

Even cared for. It might only be a job for him, but for her, his presence was reassuring and comforting.

Chapter 6

During the ferry ride, Cullen did his best to keep the conversation lighthearted, but his attempt failed. Anna's body language remained closed and stoic. He had no doubt she dreaded visiting both of their destinations. Her unique set of problems intrigued him, but he was certain he'd be able to discover information to ease her mind.

He'd already conducted a quick internet search on the Nachwelt Foundation which revealed it offered grants to worthy scientists and funded a variety of research programs. However, FARA wasn't listed as one of their recipients, which Cullen found strange since Claire had a connection to both entities.

A quick background check on FARA revealed only perfunctory information on their website. The average citizens would probably have found the basic details they were looking for, such as description of their services, a brief history, board of directors, but Cullen was familiar enough with legitimate corporate sites to know there was a whole lot more to the company than they advertised.

Next on his agenda would be to use his specialized skills to delve deep into the Nachwelt Foundation and

FARA. As yet, he hadn't divulged his findings to Anna. He'd wait until they'd visited her mother's office.

Anna had provided the address for the condo on Western Avenue, a dozen or more blocks to the left of the ferry dock. Cullen maneuvered through the honking traffic and arrived at the building a little after nine. "An impressive location."

"I'm not surprised. Mother liked...loved all things expensive." Anna climbed out of his Jeep before he could open her door.

They rode the elevator to the top floor, all the while Anna jiggled a set of keys. The first key she tried didn't work, but the second unlocked the condo. A panoramic view of the city and waterfront spread before them. "Whew." He did a three-sixty to include the loft behind him. "This must have set your mother back a dollar or two. When did she buy it?"

"Ten years ago. I'll search upstairs while you look around here."

"Fine." He watched her ascend the metal staircase, her leather sandals making soft little squeaks. She wore a deep pink sundress that set off her blonde curls and accentuated her slim figure. Anna couldn't have worn a dress if they rode his old Harley.

Cullen pivoted. *Stick to the job.* He headed for a desk in the corner which displayed a crystal container filled with pens and pencils. No computer. Next, he sorted through each drawer. Since Anna wasn't aware of this place until recently, he doubted her mother hid anything. He did locate three empty files bearing the name Frank Ahn Research Associates. Next, he removed books from a shelf one-by-one and flipped through the pages. A piece of paper listing names protruded from a large atlas. He scanned the list of twelve names, many seemed to be of German origin.

In the kitchen, he searched through the drawers and even cabinets. Obviously, Claire didn't spend much time cooking. There were few dishes and only a couple of pots and pans. Her small pantry contained cans of soup, an unopened box of crackers, and a bag of peppermints, and when he opened her refrigerator, he was surprised to find it empty. A faint odor of bleach remained as if someone disinfected the interior.

At that moment, Anna descended the stairs. "I found nothing that will help us. No laptop and no phone. How about you?"

Cullen showed her the files and the list he'd discovered. "Someone has been here since Claire passed away. The refrigerator is empty and spotless. I expected to find a container of soured milk, at least. And maybe that same person removed items that were in these files and took her computer and phone"

Sighing, Anna hitched herself onto a stool at the counter. "That's possible. Mother first showed symptoms of organ failure two months ago, but I wasn't informed right away. When she was too sick to go to the office, she stayed at her house on Bainbridge Island. Her parttime housekeeper called me the end of April. I went to see Mother, but she cut the visit short by minimizing her illness. A week later, she was hospitalized with catastrophic organ failure. I visited her once before she passed away."

Not sure how to interpret Anna's cold tone, Cullen held back any response. She was probably still overwhelmed by all she'd discovered about Claire.

Anna hiked a shoulder. "I'm sure Mother's boss

was aware of her situation and probably sent her secretary or a FARA colleague here to remove anything company related. And the milk." She smiled. "Mother did like milk in her hot tea."

"That sounds likely. Are you ready to leave?"

"Yes." Anna slid off the stool and collected her purse.

"Do you want to take anything from the condo?"

She shook her head, her hair flowing around her shoulders. "If I hadn't detected Mother's signature floral perfume in her bedroom, I would think she'd never been here. To me, this place looks as if it came furnished. Nothing here reminds me of her. She preferred antiques and rich colors. Muted grays and glass and metal weren't her style."

Cullen checked his watch. "The company offices open at ten. We'll be right on time."

Their destination was only a few blocks away. No wonder Claire chose that condo. He had a difficult time finding a parking spot, but finally pulled into a place along the curb. "Do you want me to enter with you, or should I snoop by myself?"

"Please come with me. I've never met anyone from Mom's business, and I'm not sure how they'll respond to my request to see her office." She gave him the once over and smiled. "Your presence will add clout to my humble appeal."

"Happy to oblige." He set his hands on his hips and flexed his biceps and pecs, the movements plainly visible under his cotton shirt. Her eyes widened and she lowered her head and grinned.

He wasn't usually so informal with clients, but Cullen was glad to see a playfulness under Anna's stern exterior. After they signed in at the security desk, they were buzzed through the turnstiles and then escorted to Dave Patterson's office on the fifth floor. The tall, bearded man who was Claire's former supervisor, met them at his door and proffered the requisite condolences, but his tight expression seemed to indicate he had little more to say.

"I...I'd like to see my mother's office, please." Anna stared up at him, shoulders back and chin out.

Good. She displayed a confident attitude.

"It's the least you can do for a grieving daughter." Anna might not have agreed with Cullen's words, but she allowed him to stand behind her with his arm around her small waist. He gave Patterson his meanest scowl.

"Sure. We've already packed up Claire's personal items which are in the office. It's not occupied at the moment, but you'll have to be escorted. Hold on a minute." Patterson nodded toward his office manager. "Sylvia, please accompany these folks to Claire's former office. They can take the boxes, and then call security to escort them out."

"Thank you, Mr. Patterson." Cullen dropped his arm as Anna stepped forward.

"Yes, thank you." She hesitated. "Do you need any information from me?"

"No. Your mother took care of all the necessities when she first took ill." He paused, frowning. "At which time she also informed us she had a child. We were all surprised. Goodbye." He entered his office and closed the door.

Noting the tears in Anna's eyes, Cullen took her hand and gave it a gently squeeze. She blinked and turned her head.

Sylvia motioned for them to follow her down the carpeted hall where she unlocked a door on the left. "Take as long as you need. I, uh, liked your mother." The amply proportioned secretary opened the door and stepped aside for them. The ends of her short platinum-blonde hair were dyed hot pink which matched her blouse. She attempted to button her white suit jacket over her ample bust, but gave up and walked away, leaving behind whiffs of vanilla and citrus.

Without hesitation, Cullen closed the door and pulled Anna into a hug. "I'm sorry. Why would your mother keep your existence a secret from her employer?"

She pushed back and shook her head. "I have no idea, but her actions explain a lot. No wonder she never invited me to visit."

"I can tell you're hurt. Do you want to leave?"

"Not without her belongings."

Two boxes sat at the end of a conference table. While Anna examined the consents, Cullen moseyed around the office studying the titles of books on a shelf and flipping through folders on a credenza. He found nothing of interest to help them in their quest. The immaculate desktop displayed only one nonstandard item—the brass nameplate. He held it up to show Anna. "Executive Director of Genetic Research. Claire did have a responsible job."

"I suppose." Her voice was devoid of emotion. She shoved the lid on the second box. "I'm done. As to be expected, no photographs of me, but also none of my dad. It's almost as if we didn't exist in her business life." Anna slipped her purse strap over her shoulder then picked up the box. "Let's go."

He grabbed the other box, opened the door, and beckoned Sylvia standing a few feet away. "Thanks, Sylvia. Before we leave, I have a question. We've not found Mrs. Taylor's laptop or cell phone. Did she leave them in her office?"

"The computer belonged to FARA, and I didn't find a phone when I packed her things. Sorry."

"Okay. We're ready."

By the time they reached the bank of elevators, a security guard had arrived and accompanied them to the ground floor.

"Where's the restroom?" Anna smiled at the guard and set the box on a padded bench.

He indicated the location, watched her enter, then returned to the front desk.

Cullen sat on the bench and admired the three-story foyer. Aware the guard kept a watchful eye on him, he casually studied everything in view. Large metal calligraphy letters spelled out *Frank Ahn Research Associates* on the wall above the security desk. All seemed above board and normal for a large company.

He glanced at the prominent and ornate clock above the entry doors. Anna had been gone ten minutes. He was about to check on her when she appeared and strode toward him.

"Sorry I took so long." She picked up a box and headed for the turnstiles, her actions curbing conversation.

Cullen nodded to the guard as he buzzed them through.

Curious about the smug expression on Anna's face, Cullen stowed the boxes in the back of his Jeep and asked, "What's going on?"

Anna allowed him to open her door, then jumped in and buckled her seatbelt. He hurried to his seat and started the engine. "Well?"

"There was a nervous-looking young women in the restroom and we struck up a conversation. She asked if I had come to interview for a job, as she had. Seems the company is hiring several entry-level research assistants."

He stopped at a red light and automatically glanced in the rearview mirror. "Why is that important? Do you know someone who would qualify?"

Anna burst out laughing. "Me! I don't have any experience, but my degrees are in biology and chemistry." She pulled a piece of paper from her purse. "The woman gave me the name of the HR person to contact for an interview."

Risky, but innovative. "Would being Claire's daughter help or hinder the plan?"

"Other than Sylvia and Mr. Patterson, I doubt anyone in the company knows who I am. And remember, she only recently informed her boss of my existence. Besides, Mother used her maiden name."

Cullen glanced in the rearview mirror again. The same maroon SUV he'd noticed earlier was still behind him. Not a problem unless the driver followed them to the ferry. No need to worry Anna. He looked at her and grinned. "I couldn't have devised a more brilliant plan. With you on the inside we should be able to find out a lot more about the company."

"Right. The work Mother did, and maybe how she accumulated her wealth." Anna glanced at him. "Have you discovered anything about the Nachwelt

Foundation yet? I'm interested in any connection she may have."

He explained what he'd found. "I'm surprised FARA wasn't listed as one of their recipients."

"At least mother's money will support worthy candidates." Anna slipped on a pair of sunglasses. "Oh, another interesting tidbit I learned from the young woman. The research facility isn't in Seattle. It's near Quilcene."

"On the Olympic Peninsula. Hmm. There's no mention of an alternate location on the website." He turned right toward the ferry-only lane, and the SUV turned, also. Too late for Cullen to undertake creative driving and lose the guy.

By now, Anna had noticed his preoccupation and glanced into her side mirror. "Are we being followed?"

"I think so. Nothing unusual in taking this route if you're heading to the pier, but he passed a couple of cars to stay behind us." Cullen took his place in line at one of the ticket booths for the Bainbridge Island ferry. However, the driver behind him pulled to the side and stopped. "He knows where we're headed and obviously doesn't want to join us. Too bad, because, once on the ferry, I could have confronted him." With nowhere to run, the guy wouldn't have stood a chance.

"I memorized his plate number." Anna used the piece of paper the woman had given her and scribbled down the information.

"Good. I'd memorized it too." Their line to board the ferry began to move. "Keep a look out for the SUV. He might change his mind."

The efficient loading procedure soon had the vehicles on board. Parked on the upper starboard deck,

Cullen hadn't been able to see the last cars that drove onto the ferry. He opened his door. "Stay here, please, while I check for his SUV."

Anna nodded. "Be careful."

A common admonition, but her sincere words pleased him no end. Some drivers hadn't killed their engines yet. The wind had picked up and swirled exhaust fumes around him as he strode between the rows of vehicles on the upper and lower starboard and port decks and then the main deck. The maroon SUV occupied the last spot in the middle row. As Cullen approached, the man behind the wheel tried to shrink down. No easy feat for a person of his apparent size. But a sign he was no ordinary ferry passenger.

Cullen stopped by his open window, arms folded. "Why are you following me?"

"I'm not." The bald man leaned away as far as possible.

"You've been behind me ever since I left the office building. I find that suspicious." He rested his forearms on the opening and glared at the guy. "Did Mr. Patterson send you?"

"Patterson? No."

"Who, then?"

"It...it's not what you think. Yes, I'm following you, but—"

Banging on the door, Cullen scowled. "If you don't tell me what's going on, I'll haul you out of there." Not that he would, but the threat usually worked.

The man's shoulders sagged.

"Do you work for Frank Ahn Research? What's your name?"

"I used to work for them." He hesitated, then added,

"My name's William Blake. You met my daughter this morning. Sylvia. She told me Claire Taylor's daughter came by. I need to talk to her, but you drove off before I had the chance."

An unexpected statement. "What's your business with Miss Taylor?" He had no idea if employees knew Anna did not share her mother's last name, so why advertise?

William attempted to cross his arms then grabbed the steering wheel. "I'll only confide in her."

"Fine. There's a gas station a block from the ferry dock. We'll meet you at one of the picnic benches outside."

"Thanks."

Cullen backed away, eyeing William the whole time. If he was genuine, he might provide insight which could help Anna and her cause.

Chapter 7

Although interested but skeptical of the information William shared, Anna drew in a deep breath of air redolent with recently mowed grass. Cullen had asked all the questions so far, and she was content to let him continue.

"When did you take early retirement?"

William ran a hand over his bald pate. "A year ago. I'd been the head maintenance officer for a long time. After my arthritis spread to my knees and hands, I couldn't work without pain. I received a healthy severance package and don't want to jeopardize that, but when Mrs. Taylor died suddenly, Sylvia voiced her concerns to me."

"How long has she been employed there?"

"Three, four years. She was offered this job after Patterson's predecessor and his office manager died eight months ago."

Anna jumped in before Cullen opened his mouth. "They died at the same time?"

Nodding, William massaged his right wrist.

His dark eyes held the same warmness Anna had noticed in Sylvia's.

"Otto Nelson had been with the company for

decades. His illness hit him unexpectedly, and one evening, he took an overdose of...something, and so did Ina Kendall."

Anna digested the information as she sipped her soda. "More sudden deaths in the company. The coincidences are piling up."

Elbows on the wooden table, William clasped his hands together. "That's what I need to share with you. Over the last year, at least nine long-time employees have died. My limited investigation revealed all deaths came on quickly. The person developed a major problem, such as kidney failure or a severe heart attack, then died weeks later."

"Like my mother."

"Yes. Sylvia described her decline in detail. She said Mrs. Taylor's personality even changed. She became more friendly and open, so her death hit my daughter harder than the others."

An unseen hand constricted around Anna's heart. Why hadn't her mother's attitude changed toward *her*? Guilt tightened the hold. Anna hadn't visited immediately or called when the housekeeper told her Claire was ill. She hung her head and swallowed over the pain in her throat. Too late to change her past.

"That's not all," William said. "FARA have their headquarters in Seattle, but their main research facility is near Quilcene."

"Have you been there?" Cullen turned to a blank page in his notepad.

"Only once, years ago. They had a major problem with the air circulation system. Tight security, as you can imagine. That was before the strange deaths so I didn't observe as much as I wish I had. A couple of things I noticed—several employees spoke German and there were two large portraits in the lobby. I didn't get a close look, but I'm sure one was of Mrs. Taylor."

"My mother?"

"Yes. I just caught a glimpse of the pictures and thought it odd because although she was in management, she wasn't the top-dog, so to speak."

Cullen tapped on the table. "That is unusual, but—"

"Sorry. I'm getting sidetracked. I'm not sure of the numbers, but many of the key employees at that facility have died, too. Sylvia says that's pretty much all Patterson does these days is move people around to fill vacancies as they can't hire replacements quickly enough."

Anna glanced at Cullen. Her plan to apply for a job there looked more and more promising, and if hired, she could inquire about the portrait. "Can you share anything else with us, William?"

He shook his head. "But Sylvia keeps me updated."

While removing a business card from his pocket, Cullen also withdrew the slip of paper he'd found in Claire's condo and held it out to the man. "Do you recognize any of these names?"

William scanned the list. "Yes. I paid close attention when Sylvia mentioned the employees who've recently died. Jaeger, Mason, Avery, Gerber, Jackson, Gruber, and I think Vogel."

"That's helpful." Cullen gave William his card. "As you can tell, I'm assisting Anna with her mother's affairs. Contact me if you find out additional details, especially the names of other employees who died recently."

"Certainly. Give me the paper and I'll provide my

phone number if you need to reach me." He wrote his number on the back of the page and returned it to Cullen. "When Sylvia called, she said Miss Taylor and her boyfriend were in the office. I'm glad you're helping."

"He's not—" Anna cut her sentence short as Cullen set his arm around her shoulders and squeezed.

"Naturally. My sweetheart's peace of mind is my top priority." He drew her closer.

The rumble of traffic on the road and the squawk of seagulls all merged into one blurry, distant hum. Nestled against Cullen's side provided warmth and security Anna had not experienced in many years. Not since Grant...

She pushed away, turned to Cullen and blinked. For a brief nanosecond, she wished he was her beau, but then she shook her head and landed back in reality when he removed his arm and William grinned at her. Anna cleared her throat. "Do you think Sylvia would mind if we call her occasionally?"

"Probably not, but let me check with her first. She has to be careful. I'll text you her cell number if she agrees."

"Great." Cullen pointed to his card still in William's hand. "If you need to talk, please use my contact details. I don't want anyone to bother Anna unnecessarily." He nudged her with his elbow.

"Yeah." She rolled her eyes and let out a big sigh. "All this is overwhelming. I'm grateful my Cully is so supportive."

Frowning and mouth gaping, Cullen stared at her.

His expression almost sent her into a fit of the giggles.

"Um, I'd better leave now to catch the next ferry." William pocketed Cullen's card and stood. "I didn't mean to scare you, but I'm glad we met."

"Thank you for sharing. We'll keep you updated, too." Anna waved as he climbed into his SUV.

After William drove away, Cullen drained his juice bottle. "I need to clarify several items. We won't keep him informed, because at this point, I'm not willing to trust anyone connected to your mother. We give no one your contact details. Everything has to come to me first."

"Okay. I understand. There's more?"

"Yeah. Are you all right with William and Sylvia assuming we're a couple? The charade might prove useful as I investigate further. Especially if you are hired at the research facility."

"I'm unattached." The words hung in the air and weighed heavy on her shoulders.

"Same here. Sorry, I didn't mean to snoop." He stood. "Let's get going. I know a farm-to-table bistro in Poulsbo where we can have lunch. I'm starving."

"Sure." If nothing else came of her association with Cullen, she might end up with healthier eating habits. She deposited the trash in the nearby can and headed to his Jeep. As she reached for the door handle, his hand covered hers.

"I can tell my question hit a nerve. We'll be working closely for a while, and anything you tell me is confidential, same as with Jerome." He gazed into her eyes then opened the door.

Belted into her seat, Anna hung her head as he climbed in beside her. She had never been so affected by a person's gaze before. His dark eyes emitted warmth and sincerity that seemed to penetrate her outer shell. As he eased the vehicle onto the road, she said, "I'll tell you about my last boyfriend only because you might understand me better. The knowledge probably won't help with your inquiry into Mom's business." *Really, Annika? Your attraction to him is not part of the reason?*

"If you want to."

"I met Grant Pomeroy at university where he was also an art major, and although we discussed marriage, we weren't officially engaged. I loved his zest for life, but his impulsiveness led to his death. He was killed during a skiing trip up north, Mount Baker area. Friends say he left the marked trail on a dare and tumbled over a ridge into a ravine and died on impact." She hadn't shared his tragic fate with anyone for a long time. Describing the event still cut through Anna's defenses. She folded her arms tightly about her middle and slowly inhaled and exhaled.

Cullen didn't seem to notice and asked, "How long ago?"

"Five years. We shared so much. Our major field of study, the old master artists we appreciated. I haven't had a serious relationship since. Establishing my art institute has taken up all my time and energy." She paused, then turned to him. "And you? I don't see a ring on your finger?"

"This is not about me."

"Yes, it is. You started this personal questioning bit. So, dish."

"If you insist."

"I do." Making light of the conversation helped Anna calm down.

He slowed at the entrance to the bistro parking lot. "My romantic life in a nutshell. I'm single. The eldest of four kids with three married sisters who are always on my case. Although they live in Idaho, my home state, they try to set me up on dates at every turn."

Anna looked at him. Muscular and handsome for sure, but he exuded strength of character, too. She could imagine women swooning at his feet. Maybe his 'singleness' was not for lack of prospects but his choice. And there had to be a reason. "Have you ever had, uh, you know, been in…" Why was she tripping over her tongue?

"Yes." He parked, removed the ignition key, and sighed. "I have been in love." His normal deep voice held a note of sadness.

A couple of crows landed on a fence post and cawed. Anna waited for Cullen to open his door, but he stared at the birds as if mesmerized.

"Are you ready to go in?" She unbuckled her seatbelt.

"Not yet. I'll give you a brief version of my story. I've always been interested in technology and by the time I reached junior high, I could hack into almost any account. I played awful pranks, even on my pals. One such episode of posting doctored photos on social media accounts led to a friend being rejected by the US Marines. That, and his celiac disease, which I didn't know about at the time."

Cullen paused for so long, Anna thought he'd changed his mind. "You don't have—"

"I must continue. Reed dropped out of school. We learned he worked odd jobs, but eventually ended up living on the streets and died of hyperthermia right before his twentieth birthday. I blame myself for his death."

He continued his scrutiny of the birds. "I met Krissy Laing at University, and we got engaged after graduation. Unbeknownst to me, she was Reed's cousin, and when she found out I was the guy partly responsible for his rejection and therefore his lifestyle and death, she dumped me."

"That was harsh."

"I don't blame her." His words gushed out as if he wanted the speech over with as quickly as possible. "I was a selfish, egocentric teen, and up until that incident, I didn't care what harm my mischief caused. When I heard of Reed's death I turned my life over to Jesus, and I have tried to atone for my misdeeds ever since. I use my tech skills now to help people, and never cross the legal line." He snapped a braided band on his wrist. "This is my constant reminder." *Thwack.* Another snap.

His confession drained the life out of his body. Shoulders slumped, head lowered, he appeared to wither. Then, as if inflated by a pump, he straightened, puffed out his chest and sighed. "A long time ago. Five years." He smiled at Anna. "Please, never call me Cully. That was Krissy's nickname for me."

Anna acknowledged his request with a nod then focused on her intertwined fingers to absorb the details he'd shared. No wonder his lesson the previous week on forgiveness had been powerful.

As if following her train of thought, he opened his door and asked, "Are you coming to our Bible study this evening?"

Clutching her purse close, Anna climbed out of the Jeep. "Will you be conducting the lesson again?"

"Yes. Accepting God's grace is one of the hardest things a Christian has to do. I speak from personal experience."

They walked side-by-side toward the entrance. "I'll be there."

Chatter from patrons on the shaded patio greeted them.

"We have a lot in common." He shoved his hands into his pockets. "Both of us suffered a broken relationship five years go. Now we focus on our work. Two peas in a pod."

Anna began to giggle as she took in his expansive chest, his wavy, dark hair, his sternly handsome face. "If you were in a pod, there'd be no room for any other peas."

"I can't help it if your diet is unhealthy."

"I take that as an insult." She slapped his rock-hard shoulder.

"Careful. You'll hurt yourself."

Still giggling, she nursed her stinging hand. But the thought of sharing an intimate space with Cullen sobered her instantly.

Chapter 8

"I received a cancellation not thirty minutes ago. Can you come for an interview tomorrow at two?"

Anna gulped. "Yes. Thank you, Mrs. Hays."

"I'll email the application. Bring it tomorrow along with supporting documents."

"Certainly. I look forward to meeting you." Anna ended the call and fell back among the pillows on her bed. Anxious to get involved, she had called the Human Resources number after Cullen brought her home, never expecting an appointment so soon. Now she had to collect all the required documentation. Where had she stashed college transcripts, assistantship reports, and references? She drained her mug of peppermint tea, but the residual aroma did little to calm her.

She scampered off the bed and searched in one closet after another, and finally located the box under a table in the spare room she used as her studio. Standing at the table, she removed the box's dusty lid and stared at the contents as a wave of nostalgia enveloped her. Items from her childhood bedroom included a baby doll her father gave her, photos of school friends, and a stack of picture books. She cradled them to her chest. After Papa died, no one ever read them to her again.

Near tears, Anna set aside the books and unearthed a fat envelope that contained the documents she sought. She swiped away the tears and printed the application.

Seated at her round dining room table, Anna completed the lengthy form, frequently referring to copies of transcripts, proof of assistantships, and letters of recommendation. No fabrication required, not even to the question, 'Do you have a family member employed at FARA?' No. Mother was no longer an employee.

By the time Anna had everything in order it was past seven. Too late to attend the Bible study. She texted Cullen and explained the situation, then opened her refrigerator. With his words about her diet ringing in her ears, she skipped the frozen pizza and made a chef salad instead with a light dressing of olive oil, vinegar, and seasoning. Savoring the tangy concoction, she wondered if Cullen should review her paperwork, create a false history for her. But then she recalled him saying he wouldn't cross the legal line. Maybe FARA was desperate enough to hire her although her documents weren't current.

While checking the application one last time, her phone rang. Cullen.

"I'm sorry you couldn't meet with us this evening, but I'm excited about the interview. Good for being proactive. I'm coming with you."

Anna beamed. She'd hoped he would join her. "I'll drive this time."

"Fine. I'll come by around ten to check your documents. Make sure there's nothing to connect you to Claire."

"Thanks. See you then."

~

The next morning, instead of filling up on donuts, Anna made an omelet. Would Cullen approve? She took a bite. It wasn't as if she was trying to impress him.

Small glass of cranberry juice in hand, she traipsed into her bedroom where she already had the only tailored outfit she possessed spread on the bed. A short-sleeved, baby-blue business suit. She drained her glass, brushed her teeth, then pulled her hair straight back and proceeded to create the perfect chignon like Mother's. William's mention of a portrait of someone who resembled her nagged at Anna. She ran to her studio, grabbed a tube of yellow acrylic paint, wet a washcloth then applied a little diluted color on the white streak in hair. Passable, as long as no one touched it.

Tendrils sprayed into submission and her glasses in place, Anna examined her reflection. Yup. She did not look like the Anna Knight who visited FARA yesterday. After clipping on silver teardrop earrings, she dabbed her favorite perfume on her wrists and décolletage. The crisp notes of jasmine and clementine always reminded her of a tropical summer vacation.

As she buttoned her jacket, the rumble of a motorbike engine in her short driveway shook her front window. Her heart pitter-pattered. The thought of the interview or seeing Cullen again?

Whatever. She took a deep breath then opened the door before he knocked. "Good morning. You're early."

"Whoa." Mouth gaping, he gave her the once over. "Who are you?"

"My version of a disguise. Glasses instead of

contacts, hair up, and *voilà*. What do you think?"

"Impressive. How about your paperwork?" He entered and walked straight to the dining table where she'd placed her leather attaché case. Hands on her hips, she followed him. He didn't react as much as she'd hoped.

Cullen set his helmet and a computer bag beside her case, then removed the documents and studied each one. "I see you listed Lexie as a personal reference. Is that wise? Have you told her what you're doing?"

"No, but I needed a contact from my present life. I also listed Dr. Faulkner. He was my assistantship supervisor at university. I called him yesterday, and he is willing to vouch for my scientific knowledge and good character. How much should I tell Lexie?"

Straddling a chair at the table, Cullen stroked his chin. "I know her and Tom well, and I'd trust them with my secrets."

"Are they aware you work for Jerome?"

"Yes, however, I'd advise you to tell as few people as possible what you're really up to. You've heard of plausible deniability? That way no one has to lie for you." He tapped her application. "And I assume you haven't lied on here? Lies will get you into trouble every time."

"No lies, but not every detail of my life, either. For instance, I didn't mention my art institute. I stated I sell my paintings to earn money. Which is true, but—"

"Sounds reasonable. Stick to the truth as much as possible. Of course, there's always the possibility they'll do a deep dive into your past."

"In which case I doubt they'll hire me."

"That's a risk you'll have to take."

"Will you come into the building with me?" Anna stacked the papers together and slid them back into the attaché.

"No. You can drop me off around the corner and I'll stay out of sight, but I want to be on hand in case anything goes awry."

His answer acted like a warm shawl across her shoulders. "Thank you. I'll get my billfold and keys." She retreated to her bedroom and took the items from her purse. No sense carrying two bags.

Cullen stood in the middle of her living room, gazing around. "Nice place you have."

"Renting at the moment. It's small but suits my needs." She jiggled the keys and grabbed the attaché. "My car's in the carport." She led the way through the kitchen to the back door and outside.

He took one look at her two-door sedan and shook his head. "I'll squeeze myself in there just this once. From now on, we take my Jeep."

Suppressing a giggle, Anna snapped her seatbelt as Cullen sat with his knees almost touching his chin. "Agreed. But at least if anyone sees me arrive, I'll be alone."

During the ride to the ferry dock, their conversation covered lighthearted topics, but once underway, Cullen suggested Anna call Lexie to tell her someone from FARA might call.

Anna checked the time then drew her cell phone from her pocket. "She's on her lunch break." Seconds later, Lexie answered. Anna explained Cullen was helping her sort out problems with her mother's estate. "I'm applying for a parttime job and would rather not go into details at present, but I put you down as a character reference. If someone calls, please don't mention that we operate the art institute together, or anything about my mother."

"Sounds intriguing, but if that's what you want."

"I promise I'll divulge all when I can." Anna glanced at Cullen and almost added they were on their way to Seattle. Then she recalled *plausible deniability.* "I might not be able to visit much for a while. Please trust me, Lexie, my friend."

"I will, and I'll pray for a successful conclusion."

"Thanks, and bye." Swallowing to ease the desert in her throat, Anna slipped the phone into her case. Knowing someone prayed for her added to her sense of security.

"Lexie will do right by you." Cullen patted her shoulder. "Now I want to tell you what I've discovered."

"Will your research be hampered by not having access to Mother's laptop or cell phone?"

"I'd like to see her call history, read her email exchanges, and check what websites she visited, but I have numerous tech tools to use."

"Sorry I interrupted."

"I was surprised to find that several companies in Europe and the USA conducted genetic research pre- and post-WWII."

"I recall some details from my undergraduate work." She paused. "Let's not forget that hundreds, maybe thousands of people over the years have benefitted from this research. However, considering Mother's secrecy concerning her role, I have a gut feeling much of FARA's work might not be condoned by medical authorities."

"I agree. I discovered the company was really founded in the 1940s in Germany, not in Seattle in 1969 as stated on their generic site. I traced them through numerous bogus corporations. That right there is indicative of questionable activities, but I found nothing illegal yet. However, I've only conducted a preliminary investigation."

"If I get the job, what chance do you think I have of discovering information you can't locate online?"

"A lot will depend on where you work in the facility. Oh, and I suggest you don't let on you speak German. Not today nor later."

The ferry began to slow as it neared the pier. Anna fastened her seatbelt. "I'm excited, but also apprehensive. What if…?"

Cullen grasped her hand. "Relax and act naturally."

If only it was that easy. She glanced out the window and focused on the skyline.

"Don't overplay your hand or ask too many questions. Stress your scientific background. That's your biggest asset. You know they are desperate, and you are the perfect candidate." He squeezed her hand then released it. "I'll proffer more advice if, rather, when you get the job."

She started the engine as the line of cars in front of her moved forward. "Thanks. I feel better now."

"I'd like to pray."

Turning onto the main drag, Anna smiled. "Go ahead."

"Father God, You hold our lives in Your hands. Please bless Anna today and show us the path we should take to resolve the issues that trouble her about her mother. In Jesus name. Amen."

Blaring car horns and the rumble of tires over tarmac swarmed into the vehicle. Anna closed the window. "Thanks."

"An internet search showed a coffee house around the corner from FARA. Drop me there and I'll conduct more research while you're gone. I piggyback on their wi-fi so my searches are harder to trace. And I want to compose a new worship song that's been buzzing around my heart for a few days."

What an enigma. Deep technical research and composing a worship song. All in a day's work. He was the most unusual man she'd ever met.

"By the way, you look professional and…beautiful. And I like your perfume. Makes me think of my time in Hawaii."

After Anna dropped off Cullen, she parked along the street and slid her debit card into the meter. One and a half hours. Should be enough time. Attaché case in hand, she entered the building, basking in Cullen's compliments. A different guard stood at the turnstiles today. He checked her ID then pointed the way to the HR department across the foyer to the right.

At five after two, Mrs. Hays called Anna into her office. The woman began by asking general questions and taking notes, but when she scanned the college transcripts and assistantship reports, Anna could almost see her antennae twitch.

Mrs. Hays pursed her lips then nodded at Anna. "Very impressive course work, grades, and testimonies from your mentors. However, there's no record of you pursuing this scientific avenue. That concerns me."

Anna had rehearsed her answer to such a query, but now faced with the reality of the job interview, she stammered and almost blurted out the truth—Mother never believed she could cut it in the scientific world. Just in time, Anna recalled her prepared response. "I always had a passion for painting, and I thought I could make a living as an artist." She chuckled and shrugged. "Sure, I've sold enough artwork to put a roof over my head, but I realize that was a phase I'll be glad to put behind me. I want to return to my original love of the scientific world, especially research." Warmth rose up her neck to her cheeks. Another lie. "There are numerous breakthroughs in medicine and genetic editing. And gene patenting. I want to be part of this new frontier." Even if Mrs. Hays wasn't impressed with her reply, Anna was. She almost preened in the chair.

Folding her arms, Mrs. Hays stared at Anna as if peering through her façade.

Anna sat still, clutching her attaché case, and tried not to melt under the woman's hot gaze. She swallowed but didn't lower her head. *I can play this game, too.*

Seconds dripped by like cold molasses.

Mrs. Hays raised an eyebrow. "How do you know about gene editing and patenting if you're not actively engaged in the field?"

"I do read the journals, especially articles by my mentor, Dr. Harold Faulkner." No lie. Anna did read his online articles yesterday.

Then Mrs. Hays smiled. "We'll get back to you as soon as we can. Hired or not, we'll phone you."

"Thank you for the opportunity."

"Although you lack practical experience, I'm impressed with your credentials." Mrs. Hays stood. "One thing to keep in mind, our research facility is not in Seattle."

Acting suitably surprised, Anna rose and asked, "Where is it?"

Mrs. Hays opened her door. "Put it this way, you won't have to ride the ferry."

"That's good."

"Oh, and the next orientation class begins Monday. If hired, will you be available?"

"Yes. Thanks again." Anna shook the woman's hand, and, shoulders back, walked down the hall.

Surely Mrs. Hays wouldn't have provided those details if she didn't think Anna would be hired.

Chapter 9

The stress of waiting for the phone call from FARA's Human Resources department kept Cullen awake at night. Well, that, and his concern for Anna. If *he* was anxious, he couldn't imagine how she felt. Consumed by his research on her case and for another client, he hadn't had time to visit her since the interview. Although he didn't make any major discoveries about FARA, his background checks on Claire Taylor garnered a slew of worrisome details he was eager to share with Anna. Her mother's online history only began with her daughter's birth twenty-seven years ago. Before that date, Cullen found no mention of Claire in tax files, voter registrations, credit card use, or driver's license applications, items or services almost everyone used. Either he needed to include her middle name or she was in the witness protection program. Or worse, she changed her name or was involved in unsavory activities. He compiled a list of questions to ask Anna at their next meeting.

Saturday morning chores complete, Cullen selected a variety of heavy-duty classical music pieces from his playlist, set the volume high enough for his pleasure but without bothering his neighbors, and then assembled the ingredients needed for salmon pouches. Rousing chords of the Triumphal March from Aida resounded in his kitchen as he set the fish in the oven and prepared quinoa and a salad.

The timer on his smart watch vibrated, Cullen removed the baking sheet and was about to set it on the counter when a loud banging on his open kitchen door startled him enough he almost dropped the food. He pivoted. "Anna."

"Mr. Kincaid, what are those strange-looking things you baked?"

He punched a button on his iPod and the thumping music ceased. "Sorry. I get lost in the experience. Come in."

She entered the kitchen and pointed to the tray he held. "Maybe you should set that down before you get burned."

He was so enthralled at her appearance that he momentarily forgot what he was doing. She looked like a young kid dressed in denim shorts and a floral T-shirt and her hair in pigtails. He shut his gaping mouth and slid the tray onto the counter then removed the oven mitt and cleared his throat. "Care to join me for lunch?"

"It depends. I like the aroma in here. Reminds me of savory licorice, if that's possible, but I've never eaten anything cooked in paper before. What is it?"

"Salmon, and the fennel adds notes of licorice or some people say anise. All with a drizzle of olive oil mixed with Dijon mustard." Providing the list of ingredients gave him time to recover from his embarrassment.

She perched on a stool and frowned. "I thought you were a vegetarian."

"I limit my intake of red meat." He took two plates from a cabinet and set them on the counter. "But how can a person live in the Pacific Northwest and not eat fresh salmon?"

"I remember you saying you didn't like to cook."

"I don't, but that doesn't mean I can't." He removed his apron and cocked his head. "In fact, I have a reputation for being a gourmand." Using a fork, he carefully un-crimped the parchment paper pouches which released sweet- and savory-smelling steam.

"You seem to have hidden talents, but I'll reserve judgment until I've tasted your creation." Anna set her purse on the stool beside her. "Which obviously means I accept your invitation."

"Good. We can serve our plates in here then eat on the back porch." He gathered utensils and two trays and set them on the counter along with the salad bowl and saucepan of quinoa. "No fancy place settings."

She giggled. "If you came to my house we'd be having microwaved dinners. This looks interesting."

"You don't cook?" He added two glasses of iced water to the array.

"Not if I can help it. My microwave is my best friend."

"I can teach you." Why had he offered? The last thing he needed was the intimacy of one-on-one sessions with Anna. Thankfully, she only smiled at his suggestion.

Back to business. He pointed to one of the pouches and handed Anna a large spoon. "Have as much salmon as you want. I always cook large pieces so I'll have leftovers."

She took a third of a steak and added a few of the

trimmings. "Is this green stuff the fennel?"

"Yeah. The sliced bulb under the fish is tasty."

Plates piled high on their trays, Cullen followed Anna outside. Clouds hid the sun, resulting in a pleasant outdoor temperature.

Anna sat on the wooden bench and set her tray on her lap, but her knees bounced so much, she had to move the tray to the seat beside her. The action reminded Cullen of the first time he'd seen her at the Bible study evening. Then he stole a glance at her face. What a chump. He noticed the gleam in her eye and her expectant expression. She had news. "What—?"

"I got the job." She leapt off the bench. Hugging herself, she twirled then faced him. "They called about an hour ago. I tried to contact you, but you didn't answer your phone."

Cullen set his tray on the small table and stood. "Great news." He hesitated then held his arms wide, and she fell against his chest. "Congratulations." Seconds later, he released her and stepped back.

She lowered her head and returned to the bench. "Sorry. I'm excited."

"Me too. I can't wait to see what you discover at the research facility." He set his tray across his lap. "Let's pray. Father, thank You for this food and for the good news Anna received. Please protect her as she proceeds with this plan. In Jesus's name. Amen." He munched on a morsel of salmon. Perfect seasoning. "When do you start?"

Stabbing her fork into the salad, she said, "First, Mr. Gourmand, I have to say this is all delicious. You can cook food in packets for me any time."

He caught the flush creeping up her neck and into

her cheeks and grinned. Nothing he'd like more, but they had serious work to do. "The job?"

"Oh, right. Monday at nine. I printed out the orientation instructions and brought them for you to see. A long list of dos and don'ts. I have to leave my car at a designated spot in a little community called Uncas at the southern tip of Discovery Bay. It's about thirteen miles from here. Then all new hires will be driven to the facility. We can't keep any electronics with us and any notes we take have to be left in an assigned locker."

"William did say they have a strict security protocol, which is understandable." Cullen drained his glass. "Did they indicate you'll always be driven to the facility?"

"No. We have six days of orientation. I suppose we'll find out after that."

His mind raced over ways to counteract the prohibition of carrying electronics. He'd hoped Anna could take photos or make recordings. He might have to rig up something that would go undetected. "I'm sorry I don't have any dessert."

Anna rubbed her stomach. "I can't eat another bite. Thank you."

"Let's go in and read that list, and then I want to give you tips and advice."

"Sure."

They entered the kitchen and Cullen removed the plates and glasses from the trays and set all in the sink. "I'll clean up later. Come into the living room and show me your list." He indicated Anna sit on the sofa, then settled in his oversized recliner and took the sheet of paper she removed from her purse. Meticulous instructions appropriate for a place conducting research. Nothing seemed out of the ordinary.

He returned the page to her and tented his fingers. "I already advised you not let anyone know you speak German. It might not matter, but since FARA was established in Germany, and William said he heard employees there speak German."

"Good idea. That way I can listen in when no one suspects I can understand. What else?"

"Try to stay under the radar. Don't make your interest in anything but your job obvious. Sure, you want to prove your scientific knowledge, but ask questions and observe without drawing suspicion. When you get home Monday, we need to debrief."

She drew in a deep breath. "Okay. I'm excited. Nervous, too."

"If possible, make friends with the other new hires. Especially if they work in a different area. But don't share too many personal details. Keep your history as vague as possible." He shifted in the chair. "Which reminds me. I conducted in-depth research on your mother. I can't find much about her prior to your birth. Do you have a copy of her birth certificate, marriage license, passport? Any legal documents?"

"No." Anna fiddled with her purse strap. "That's strange. I never considered those documents when I searched her home office. She is becoming more and more mysterious." Her phone rang and rang. Finally, she drew it from her bag and checked the screen. "I have to take this." Rising, she answered as she walked into the kitchen. Seconds later she returned, her face ashen. "A neighbor's housekeeper called Mom's housekeeper to say she saw lights on in the house late last night. When Bonnie drove over and checked a few minutes ago, she found someone had broken into the office and ripped most of the paneling off the walls."

Cullen stood. "I'll drive." He patted his pockets for his keys and headed to the front door. "This way."

They rode in silence, Anna clutching her purse, the skintight over her knuckles, and Cullen going as fast as the speed limit allowed. Once on the island, he followed her directions to the waterfront mansion in a gated community where a white SUV waited in the circular driveway.

A middle-aged woman opened the front door and Anna ran toward the house. Cullen entered after her and tried to ignore the opulent foyer. No wonder she commented on the condo's industrial décor.

Anna introduced him then asked the housekeeper, "What's been stolen?"

"Nothing I can tell." Bonnie stopped at the open office door. "This is the only room that's been disturbed. I've worked here long enough to know nothing elsewhere in the house is missing. Even your mother's jewelry box is intact."

"Have you notified the police?" Cullen surveyed the room.

"No. I wanted to consult Anna first since I didn't know what she might have taken from the office."

Anna shrugged. "Only a few documents." She peeked into the room. "What a mess. Other than the paneling and books strewn around, everything is as I left it after my last visit."

"I assume there's no security system," Cullen said.

"Right. Mrs. Taylor did consider installing one but never got around to making the call."

"How did the intruder get in?"

"Well, this might be my fault. He broke the side window of the garage and came through the door into the kitchen. I seldom go into the garage, but I, uh, must have forgotten to lock it." Hanging her head, Bonnie sighed.

"No. That was probably me." Anna bit her bottom lip. "I came here last week and peeked into the garage."

Cullen turned to Bonnie. "Did you enter the office or touch anything?"

"No."

"Good." He placed his hand on Anna's shoulder. "Before I go in, you need to decide if you want to call the cops."

"The person was obviously looking for something specific, and if nothing has been taken from the rest of the house, then let's wait. At this point I'd rather not involve the authorities."

Cullen gave her shoulder a squeeze. With all the uncertainty surrounding her mother, he couldn't blame her. But he had to add, "Once I go in there, I'll destroy any forensic evidence the perpetrator might have left behind."

"I don't care."

"Okay. I'll arrange for the window to be replaced. While I check out the damage, please wait by the door." He stepped over the paneling pieces, insulation, and books, skirted the two armchairs, and stopped in front of the desk. He turned to survey the destruction in the windowless room. Three walls had been partially damaged. He pointed to his left. "The kitchen shares that wall." Then pointed to his right. "I assume that's an outside wall."

Bonnie nodded. "And the garage is behind you."

"Aha. The only wall not damaged is that one." He pointed to the doorway. "And I know why. It's not thick enough to conceal a safe. You can come in now. Is there a safe in the house? Seems to me that might be what the intruder was looking for."

"I have no idea." Anna dropped into one of the armchairs, a melancholy expression clouding her face.

"I don't know, either." The housekeeper moved the coffee table and sat in the other armchair. "Let me explain my situation. I've worked for Mrs. Taylor ten years or so. Obviously, I have a key and she gave me free reign anywhere in the house except this office. She kept the door locked when she wasn't in here, and I could only clean the room if she was present."

"Then, my guess would be if she has a safe it's in here." Seated at the desk, Cullen scanned the room again. Empty bookshelf askew, three framed paintings stacked against the undamaged wall, and—

"Why didn't he tear up the floor, too?" Anna asked.

"Since he only searched this room, maybe he knew it would be in here."

"That's a scary thought." She frowned and nibbled a nail.

Bonnie's cell phone rang and after checking the screen, she stood and left the office.

Motioning Anna to come close, Cullen leaned forward and whispered, "Do you trust Bonnie?"

"I have no reason not to, and Mother wouldn't have hired anyone who wasn't trustworthy. Why?"

Returning to the office, Bonnie gathered her purse. "My little granddaughter fell, and my son needs me to babysit her brother while they take her to the hospital."

"Oh, Bonnie. I'm sorry. Please go and thank you for coming to the house and for calling me. I hope her condition isn't serious."

"I'll pray for you all." Cullen remained at the desk. "Drive carefully."

"Thanks." The housekeeper hurried away. Seconds later, they heard her vehicle drive off.

"What were you saying about trust?"

Cullen turned to the wall behind him. "If there is a safe in here, I'd rather no one, not even Bonnie, know where it is." He kicked at a piece of intact paneling. "I imagine the intruder pounded on the walls, and if he heard a different sound indicating something solid behind it, ripped off sections. Obviously, without success." He tented his fingers. *Where would I hide a safe?*

Perched on the corner of the desk, Anna tilted her head at him. "What if there's no safe but a secret compartment in Mother's desk? I mean, secrecy surrounds her life, why not a good old fashioned false drawer."

Smiling, Cullen opened the center drawer a few inches. "Good idea. Let's examine them." He pulled it all the way out and felt inside the cavity but found nothing unusual. While Anna did the same to the top drawer on his left, he examined the large drawer on his right. It contained hanging files. "I suppose you went through all these folders?"

"Yes. That's where I found the deed for her condo."

Cullen slowly moved each file along the track, then one caught on a metallic projection. He ran his finger down the left side of the wooden drawer and felt what seemed to be a rounded screw head. But when he peered into the space, he noticed it was a silver button. He pressed it and an almost imperceptible click sounded behind him and to his right.

Anna looked up the same time he turned. One of the vertical panels of the undamaged wall opened a mere quarter of an inch. He stood and stared at Anna who moved around the desk.

"That's it. The intruder doesn't know how close he got." She hiked a shoulder. "Let's check it out."

Together, they stepped to the corner. "Do the honors." He nudged her arm.

Lips pressed together, eyes wide, Anna set the tips of her fingers in the fractional opening and pulled. The paneling swung open like a door and revealed a bathroom. Musty, piney disinfectant odors filtered out. Anna flipped on the light switch. "Ugh. What ugly pink tile. And paint to match. I can't imagine Mother chose this color."

Cullen smirked. "Hand sink, commode, shower cubicle. All pink. Why would she keep this room a secret? Many people have a bathroom connected to an office."

"I don't think Bonnie knew about it. She would have mentioned it otherwise, right?"

"Yeah. Maybe the safe is in here. The room seems to be the same length as the office which means the wall opposite this narrow door backs up to the garage." Cullen removed his pocketknife and began tapping on each tile, starting on the top row which in this part of the room was at his shoulder level. "It's most unusual to have tile all over. I'll check here. Find a pair of scissors or something metal and you try the tiles in the shower."

Anna hurried into the office and soon returned with a letter opener. "This is heavy. It should do the trick." She opened the glass shower door and began tapping on the lowest row of tiles. "If I was going to hide a safe in the wall, I wouldn't put it at eye level."

"That's a good point." Cullen moved to the second row of three- by six-inch garish tiles which were individually grouted. "Look for inconsistencies in the grouting."

The constant tapping echoed in the small room. Cullen worked faster on the tedious chore, and then he heard a distinct thud from the shower cubicle. He swung around.

Anna stood, hands on her hips. "I think I found it. As you speculated, the grout right here in the corner is narrower and darker. At first, I thought it might be mold, but Mother wouldn't tolerate such an insult." She tapped on more tiles, each provided the same thud.

Hovering by the open shower door, Cullen cleared his throat. To climb in with Anna would be a tight squeeze, but she showed no inclination to leave. *Focus on the job, Cullen.* "Show me." He stepped in anyway.

Anna tapped another tile close to the corner opposite the faucets. "These three." She pointed then backed up.

The rows of tiles were at knee height. He pressed the corners, the centers, even tried pressing two spots at once. After numerous attempts, he hit the right combination, and a section of the wall popped out on a rusty hinge.

A metal cavity about twelve by fourteen by eight inches occupied the exposed corner. A small, ornately carved wooden jewelry box sat on top of a thick folder tied with cord.

"I…I can't. My…my insides are all jittery." Anna covered her mouth with her hands and retreated to bathroom door. "You take them out, Cullen. Please."

"Of course. Go sit and I'll join you." He picked up the heavy jewelry box, then slid out the folder. He was not familiar with the type, but the water stains and faded cover indicated it was old.

Back in the office, he pushed the other armchair close to Anna's, sat and handed her the box.

"I don't want to see any jewelry. What's in the folder?" She set the box on the small coffee table and eyed him as if he held her fate in his hands.

A gentle tug on the cord and the folder opened. The top document, yellowed and creased, displayed handwritten data and printed script in German. He held it out to her.

Anna took it and as she read, her hands began to shake. "Birth certificate for Hugo Ritter, born December, 1901." She removed the next document from the folder. "Birth certificate for Clara Schneider, born October, 1907." She looked at him, the amber flecks in her eyes dark with dread.

"What's wrong?" He took the certificates from her trembling fingers.

Rising, Anna wiped her hands on her shirt as if to rid them of contaminants. "No, no, they can't be right."

Cullen stood, troubled by her wan face and quavering voice.

Anna closed her eyes and swayed.

Dropping the papers and the folder just in time, Cullen caught Anna as she fainted.

Chapter 10

The patting on her cheek continued and a distant voice said, "Wake up, Anna."

She swatted at her face and connected with a hand. Blinking, she stared into Cullen's eyes, filled with concern. "What happened?"

"You fainted." He knelt beside her chair. "Do you want something to drink?"

"No, thanks. What...? Ah, the documents."

"Why would birth certificates have such an affect?" Cullen picked up the papers and settled in his chair.

"I'll have to study them further, but the names bare a remarkable similarity to my parents' names." She pointed to the fancy cursive handwriting. "Ritter is German for Knight, and Schneider is German for Taylor. Hugo, Hugh, and Clara, Claire. If only their first or last names matched the translation, but both. I...I think these details are too significant to ignore."

"What about the dates? Could these people be your grand, no, great-grandparents?"

Shrugging, she melted into the cushioned chair. "That's one theory." She didn't even know the names of her grandparents. So many missed opportunities to ask her parents about their family histories. Neither had seemed interested when she broached the subject, and now she had reason to understand their hesitancy. Knots of trepidation filled her stomach. She ran to the bathroom, bent over the sink, and splashed cold water on her face.

Cullen stood at the door and pulled a small towel off the rack. "Dry your face and sit back down. You're in shock."

Face and hands dried, Anna returned to her chair. "I don't know what we've discovered, but I want to get out of here."

"I understand. I'll call my good friend Evan who runs a construction company. He'll replace the broken window today, and I recommend you install a security system."

She had no energy to respond and nodded.

"I'll take care of it all, if you like. Including the wall repairs."

Again, she nodded. "Thanks."

He secured the bathroom door, then set the birth certificates back in the folder and tied the cord. "You'd better take the jewelry box, too."

"I suppose." She dropped the box into her spacious purse and eased out of the chair. "I'll give you a spare front door key. Please get the best security system available." A giggle escaped. "Remember, money's no problem." Hurrying outside before Cullen noticed her tears, Anna clung to a pillar supporting the portico and swiped at her cheeks. She gritted her teeth and huffed out a breath trying to allay her apprehension. No wonder Mother hid the certificates. What else had she kept secret?

Cullen closed the door, accepted a key from Anna

then locked the deadbolt. "We won't be able to get anything done right away. I'll contact a couple of security companies and schedule installation as soon as possible. How about I ask Evan to stay in the house until then? His wife's out of town for a couple of weeks and he won't mind."

"Good idea. I'll tell Bonnie."

"His name's Evan Irving. He'll need a key."

"I have another spare."

During the ride back to Port Townsend, Anna's fingers itched to open the folder and examine more documents, but she wasn't sure she could conceal her bizarre fears from Cullen. She'd requested his help, but she wanted to be alone when she read the rest of the papers. Nerves coiled in her stomach at the prospect of what she'd find.

Cullen parked in his driveway. "As I said before, you've had a shock. Go home and rest. I'll pack a bag and come stay with you."

Any other time, she might have accepted his suggestion. "No, but thanks. I...I need time to decipher this lot." She patted the folder.

"Are you sure? It won't be any trouble."

His insistence almost broke through her resolve. On the verge of agreeing, the old familiar anxiety bugs gnawed at her insides. "No." She had no desire for Cullen to witness a possible meltdown. "I want to be alone when I examine the other documents." Fingers curled around the door handle, she looked straight ahead to avoid the plea in his eyes.

"Okay. Change of subject. On Sundays, I travel to little communities in the area and hold church services. Tomorrow, I'm going to Dungeness. Come with me?"

Spend time in his company and experience his strong faith firsthand? Nope. Not when she feared what she would discover about her parents, her past, her future, and then have to reconcile that truth with a God she didn't know well. And maybe lay bare her soul before this man. "Not yet. I'll call you later." Anna exited his Jeep and climbed into her car. "Thanks for lunch and your help today."

He waved as she drove away.

It would be all too easy to rely on his strength, both physical and emotional, but she had to confront the enormity of their discovery by herself. The short drive home gave her time to use her breathing techniques to calm her spirit.

Armed with a mug of hot chocolate and a notepad, Anna settled on her bed, the open folder on her lapboard along with a copy of her mother's death certificate. First, she studied the birth records. No doubt they were genuine. She noted the towns where Hugo and Clara were born and the names of their parents to look up later. But the subjects' names concerned her the most. It was not unusual for children or grandchildren to be named after their parents, but for both her mother and father to share the names on these old certificates was too much of a coincidence. And none of the four people used second names. Extraordinary, in her opinion.

Claire's death certificate listed her birth as 1967, and her mother's name as Yvonne Taylor. Claire had pre-paid funeral arrangements and must have provided these details, none of which Anna knew beforehand. She jotted down dates and concluded, age-wise, Claire could be Clara's granddaughter. But why had three generations of women maintained the same last name? She hadn't located a copy of Papa's death certificate among Mother's papers, but in light of recent discoveries, she would order one immediately.

Anna slid another document in German from the folder. A faded and creased marriage certificate for Clara and Hugo, dated 11 January, 1930, which fell in line with the dates of their births. Clara would have been twenty-three in 1930, and Hugo twenty-nine. However, the next document added to Anna's concern. A marriage certificate in English for Claire Taylor and Hugh Knight, also dated January 11, but issued by Washington State in 1990. The absurd notion they were the same people refused to dissipate, especially taking into account the identical wedding date. And why did Mother keep the older documents hidden?

Slumping among her pillows, Anna sighed. Was there some significance as to why Mother chose a wedding date exactly sixty years later than Clara and Hugo? She drained her mug then picked up a magnifying glass and studied the signatures on both licenses. Obviously, the names were different, but the handwriting did appear to be similar. An expert could tell for sure, but Anna was not ready to share these details with anyone yet. Not even Cullen or Lexie.

Only two documents remained in the folder. At a glance, Anna could tell neither were birth certificates. Why did Mother conceal birth records for Hugo and Clara, their marriage license, and the marriage certificate for Hugh and Claire, but not include their birth records? She shook her head, picked up one document and read the heading on the legal-sized paper. "Das Institut für Genforschung. The Institute for

Genetic Research." Skipping all the printed content, she focused on the signature at the bottom. Clara Schneider. And Hugo Ritter signed the last document.

Anna scanned the German text and discovered Clara and Hugo had signed contracts when they were employed at the institute, 1930 for Hugo and 1934 for Clara. Her head swarming with possibilities, Anna threw her lapboard aside and ran into the living room. Another coincidence too important to ignore. Clara and Hugo worked in genetic research. Mother had, too. What about her father?

She snatched his photograph from the mantel. All her memories of Dad were of him at home. Always available. He didn't leave the house to go to an office. He used a cane when he walked, and he had a nagging cough, but to a little girl, he was just Dad. He could have been seriously ill. In fact, Anna didn't know the cause of his death—another reason to order that certificate pronto.

Backing up to the stone fireplace surround, Anna returned Papa's picture then closed her eyes. All the while she'd examined the documents, she'd been able to control her anxiety by breathing slowly, but now the familiar parasites of fear, doom, worthlessness, coiled in her stomach, spread to her chest, and inched their way to her mind. She gasped for air as words she'd read wafted in and out of focus. About to dissolve into a puddle of uselessness, she opened her eyes. Papa's chess pieces lay beside the board on her coffee table. If he'd lived, he would have told her the truth.

Instead of collapsing to the floor, Anna drew in a breath. "I will not give in. I am stronger than my affliction." Fueled by anger at her mother for keeping so many secrets, Anna made an impulsive decision—drive to the waterfront in an effort to rid herself of the debilitating effects of her disorder before she succumbed to a full-blown assault. She packed all the papers back in the folder, tied it up and, in a state of paranoia, hid it behind her washing machine. Why not hide the jewelry box there, too? She retrieved the heavy object from her purse, contemplated opening it for a split second, then wrapped it in a dish towel and stashed it with the folder.

Purse and a light jacket in hand, she climbed into her car. On the way, she bought a burger and soda, then circled the downtown area searching for a parking spot. In spite of the gathering clouds, tourists and locals were out in force, and she finally parked two blocks away.

The paved plaza near the water teemed with pedestrians. Anna sat on the edge, her feet resting on the rocky beach. Her food had little taste, and the soda seemed flat. The wind kicked up, sending wisps of sea spray over the area. She zipped up her jacket but didn't budge. The dark, scurrying clouds promised rain and the ocean took on a steely-gray hue. The crowd dwindled until Anna and a few other stalwart souls remained. She drew her bare legs to her chest and covered them with her jacket. It might be June, but this close to the water and with the sun shrouded, the temperature dropped dramatically.

Alone on her perch, Anna reviewed the details she'd discovered in the documents. Her parents could be named after their respective ancestors and the weddings dates could be coincidences. Nothing more. She looked out across the churning water, now dark and menacing, and recalled a whale watching trip she'd taken last summer. The day started out bright and breezy, but a storm scurried in while they were two hours from shore. A pod of orcas had kept the passengers entertained, breaching, tail-slapping, and rolling around each other. One massive whale had surfaced close to the boat, his mouth agape, and although Anna had been enthralled, she clung to the rails, sure if she let go, she'd end up as bait.

Shaking off the memory, and not sure why, a cold sense of foreboding enveloped her. Gathering her trash, she stood as an absurd notion floated into her mind. If, and it was a mighty big *if*, the Hugo and Clara named in the documents were indeed the same people as her parents Hugh and Claire, then her dad had only been six years older than her mother, but he certainly looked much older. What if they'd participated in experiments with genetic modification?

She sank onto a bench. Raindrops pelted her and she raised the hood of her jacket. If any of these ideas were true, what did that mean for her? Anna had physical traits from each parent therefore certain she was their biological offspring. If their genes had been modified, how would that affect her future? Surprised she didn't revert back to crisis mode, she ran to her vehicle, saying, "Thank You, Lord. Thank You for giving me strength." Water dripping off her jacket, she climbed into her car and relaxed against the seat. She'd uttered her first prayer.

~

Sleep eluded Anna. After thrashing about in bed for hours, she rose at dawn and brewed a mug of coffee. The burden of what she'd discovered sat heavy on her shoulders and she needed help before she surrendered to the weight. Lexie had always been her sounding board, but Cullen knew about the documents. Why not call on them both?

Anna made a quick trip to the grocery store, cleaned house, and did a load of laundry. None of the chores eased her headache nor removed the knots in her stomach although she'd rested several times to utilize her calming techniques. She waited until she knew Lexie would be home from church and asked her to come over at two. Then she left a message for Cullen with the same request.

Just before two, she prepared a pitcher of lemonade and set out a fruit platter alongside her parents' papers. Lexie arrived first. Anna held back the tears as she lost herself in her friend's comforting hug.

"Hey, ladybug. Good to see you."

"Thanks for coming on such short notice." The tension in Anna's shoulders eased immediately. "I invited Cullen. In the meantime, I'll tell you why he's helping me. Let's sit at the table." During the next fifteen minutes, she explained the provisions of her mother's will and the reason she applied for a job at FARA.

"No wonder you haven't been to our art institute for a while." Lexie forked several squares of watermelon onto a plate. "You have more to share, don't you?"

Patting the documents, Anna said, "Yes. Scary stuff, but I'll wait for Cullen."

The roar of his motorbike quelled the rising panic surging through her. She gulped in air and calmly walked to the front door and opened it. His physical presence added to her composure. "I appreciate you coming."

"No problem. I heard the tension in your voice." He nodded to Lexie. "I'm glad you're here, too."

Seated opposite Cullen, Anna centered the papers in front of her on the table. Although tempted to nibble on a few succulent cherries, she sipped the sweet, tart lemonade instead. "I spent many hours reading these documents and trying to fathom what they mean. Let me give you the gist before you ask any questions."

After outlining her discoveries, Anna took another sip of lemonade, noting Lexie's raised eyebrows and Cullen's frown. "I don't know what this all means, but I think Hugo and Clara might be my parents."

"No. They can't be. That would mean..." Lexie's voiced trailed.

Cullen picked up where she left off. "That would mean their genes had been altered, modified to increase their longevity and to stop them from aging normally."

"Whoa. I don't understand." Eyes wide, Lexie held up her hands in stop gestures. "I thought our genes were determined at conception. I'm not the one with science degrees at this table, but how can you even consider changing genes in adults?"

Anna folded her arms. "Believe me, I'm as confused and as skeptical as anyone. But the information in these papers is too significant to ignore."

"If modifying genes in adults is possible, why haven't we heard about it?" Lexie's gaze darted from Cullen to Anna. "Obviously I've read about genetically modified organisms, GMOs, but—"

"You're right. Scientists have modified crops and cattle for decades, in seeds or ova, but my research into FARA provided enough data to support our opinion..." Cullen nodded toward Anna, "...that the company might be involved in nefarious activities." He paused. "GMHs. Genetically Modified Humans."

Anna rolled her eyes. "If the situation wasn't so serious, that would be funny. But back to reality. We found out a number of people who worked at FARA also died suddenly. Organ failure, just like my mother. In fact, the company is so short staffed, they hired me." Anna's little smile did nothing to lighten the atmosphere.

"I...I did give you a glowing reference, by the way, but now I'm not sure I want you to work there."

"Lexie, I know you have Anna's welfare in mind, but this is the perfect opportunity for her to find out details I have not been able to online." Cullen turned to Anna. "But you have the final say. Do you still want to go tomorrow?"

"You start that soon?" Lexie asked.

Anna nodded.

"But, ladybug, are you sure you can handle the stress?" She cocked her head in Cullen's direction, eyebrows raised.

Anna had not told Cullen about her anxiety issues yet. With a subtle hike of one shoulder, she glanced at Lexie then at him. Both were concerned about her and that aided her resolve. "I have to go. Originally, I wanted Cullen to find out how my mother accumulated her wealth and why she left half of it to the Nachwelt Foundation. If Hugo and Clara are indeed my parents, then it seems logical that if she worked in research for eighty plus years and my dad for sixty, they would have earned a bundle and would want to fund their pet projects." She shook her head. "My quest now is to discover if they were indeed my parents and what might have been done to them, and also to find out about me. Do I carry altered genes? If so, can these modifications be passed on to my children?" The very idea sent a shiver across her shoulders.

Lexie squeezed her hand. "Oh, my dear ladybug. What a burden. But I understand your need to discover the truth."

"Do you agree, Cullen?" Anna asked.

He placed his large hand over hers and Lexie's. "Yes, but your task has taken on a dangerous element. If you choose to go, you must be extra careful."

"I will." The heat from their hands radiated through her arm to her torso where it settled near her heart. Lexie, her best friend for five years, and Cullen, who was fast becoming more than her lawyer's investigator, seemed to be infusing their strength into her. "Pl…please pray for me."

"Of course, my friend."

"Absolutely."

Anna bowed her head as Lexie and Cullen placed their hands on her shoulders. She couldn't remember what they said, but she felt the presence of something much greater than three human beings.

Chapter 11

Following the detailed instructions provided by the HR department, Anna parked her car in the Ride Share lot near the little community of Uncas. Several vehicles, including a black transport van devoid of any logo, were there already. She checked the time on her cell phone—ten minutes before nine—then turned it off and placed it in the glovebox.

The door of the van opened and a tall, statuesque woman wearing a navy-blue lab coat and holding a clipboard stepped out. Anna adjusted her glasses then gathered her hair into a ponytail. A chignon was too fancy for work and needed attention to keep it neat. She checked in the rearview mirror to make sure her white streak was adequately disguised, then grabbed her billfold, the only personal item allowed, and after locking her vehicle, approached the van.

Cullen's advice echoed in her mind. Observe everything. Don't be too obvious when questioning peers, and above all, don't break the rules.

Two other people exited their vehicles and joined Anna. She recognized the young woman she'd met at FARA headquarters in Seattle and nodded, but neither spoke.

The clipboard lady smiled at them. "Good morning. I'm Judy Coates, your orientation officer." She reached into a pocket and withdrew several name tags. "You must wear your tag at all times while in the facility. These are temporary and will be replaced once you pass your training period." Holding up two, she asked the young man, "Marcus or Raul?"

"Marcus Drake, Ms. Coates." He accepted his tag but the tremors in his scrawny hands prolonged the task of clipping it to his shirt collar.

"Please call me Judy. Which one of you is Natalie?"

Natalie took the proffered tag and then Judy handed the other one to Anna.

"We run an efficient operation and require punctuality. We'll depart exactly at nine o'clock, with or without Raul." Judy pointed to the van. "You may board. Remember, no cell phones."

A flush crept up Marcus's angular face. "I forgot." He ran back to his pickup, stowed his phone and returned as a car pulled into the lot.

Tapping her foot, Judy eyed the beefy guy who exited the old sedan and approached the van. "You must be Raul."

"Yes. Sorry I'm—"

"We accept no excuses." Judy pursed her lips and sniffed the air as she gave him his tag. "Too much aftershave, Mr. Espinoza. We are a no-perfume facility. Didn't you read the instructions?"

"I...did. Sorry. It's a habit." If possible, Raul lost a couple of inches in height. "I'll wash it off when we get there."

A nod from Judy. "Everyone, take a seat, please." She entered the van after the four trainees.

Anna had always tried to be punctual. She'd arrive earlier tomorrow as she didn't want to come afoul of their orientation officer.

The driver closed the automatic door and started the engine. It made little noise and Judy's instructions could be heard loud and clear. She indicated where the trainees had to sit, then perched sideways on the front seat and faced the riders. Anna settled behind Natalie and the two men sat opposite on separate seats.

After a word from Judy, the driver pressed a button on his dashboard and a transparent panel rolled down in front of the first row of seats. The instructor waited until the panel reached the floor but did not hint at its purpose.

"I'll begin our orientation while we ride to the facility." She reached into a backpack at her feet and removed four khaki cloth bags and handed them to the passengers. Her short, dark hair had fallen across her forehead and into her eyes. She patted it back in place and in so doing, exposed her ears which protruded through the strands. An unfortunate hairstyle.

Anna gave herself a mental nudge. *Focus. Not the details Cullen needs.*

"Place your personal items in these bags. Keys, wallets, and all jewelry. You will be issued special notebooks and pens. They have security alerts imbedded so they can't be removed from the premises without raising an alarm. Take whatever notes you need, but at the end of each day, your pad and pen will be secured in your locker. You will not be allowed to take any notes with you."

"What about lunch?" Raul asked.

"We have an excellent cafeteria. When you are

accepted as an employee, you may bring your own meals." She managed a small smile. "Don't worry, you won't go hungry."

The young guy grinned and leaned back.

Judy continued. "The usual training sessions will take six days. Yes, you will come on Saturday. Our facility operates 24/7. Don't expect a nine to five, Monday to Friday job. All details which were in the introductory information. You are qualified, but personality, commitment, and dedication will be taken into consideration." She stared directly at Raul. "I hope you all make the cut. You will notice our employees wear different colored lab coats. The colors identify the areas in which they work. When vetted, you will be issued yours, along with your permanent identity badge that must be worn at all times. It is also color-coded. Each door and elevator has a card reader and a list of colors that will be admitted. If you try to enter a place you are not authorized to, security will remove you immediately from the premises and you will be fired." She looked at each rider in turn. "Understood?"

A chorus of yeses.

Anna's stomach knotted. Her quest might prove impossible. How could she snoop with limited access and strict protocols? She lifted her gaze from her hands twisting in her lap to meet Judy's dark stare. Anna cleared her throat and although every sane fiber in her being wanted to yell, "Stop the van. Let me off," she refused to lower her head and, after a few seconds, Judy turned around.

Since it seemed Judy had concluded her speech, Anna took the opportunity to assess the fellow trainees. She figured Natalie was in her mid-twenties. A redhead with a sultry voice that contrasted with her petite build. Marcus was harder to read. His lack of body mass made it difficult to gauge his age. Probably closer to thirty. His sharp features and wispy brown hair lent him a bird-like appearance.

Raul, probably the youngest member, seemed the most relaxed. He smiled at Anna and his dark brown eyes twinkled as if he shared her secret. He may have begun a conversation if she hadn't looked away.

Anna turned her attention to the highway rolling through the vibrant green forest. She hadn't traveled that way before, but a sign indicated nine miles to Quilcene. All of a sudden, the window tinting increased until she could see nothing outside and the panel behind Judy darkened, too. The other passengers noticed, and Raul posed the obvious question.

"Hey. What happened? Are we in a tunnel?"

Judy turned. "No need to worry. This is our way of ensuring the entrance to our facility is kept secret. Once you graduate from the program you can drive yourselves to work. Now sit back and relax. We'll be there in a few minutes."

The van slowed, turned right onto a bumpy track then rumbled over a cattle guard. It continued along a smoother road until it stopped at what Anna deduced was a security gate. Although the driver spoke with someone, she couldn't decipher his words. He drove on and twenty seconds later, stopped the van, and the panel rose to its place in the roof.

When the door opened, Judy stood, backpack and clipboard in hand. She descended the steps. "Follow me."

A three-story glass and steel building loomed in

front of them. Judy led the group to the main entrance. She swiped her card and the monstrous glass doors swished open. A curved reception counter about ten yards in blocked their progress. Two men took positions at either end.

"Welcome to the Frank Ahn Research Associates facility." Judy swept her arm wide, and Anna was sure she'd take a bow any second.

The four trainees' gazes followed Judy's gesture and they stared around the vast foyer. Suitably impressed, Anna turned and gasped. There above the entrance door were two huge portraits. Brass plaques under each indicated their names. Frank Ahn to the left, and Clara Schneider to the right.

Anna grasped Raul's arm as the blood drained from her head. Clara definitely could have been Mother's twin.

Chapter 12

Lyrics and score for his new worship song complete, Cullen placed his guitar in its case and stretched. His break from online research had helped clear his mind and eased his tense shoulder and neck muscles. Before he'd consumed his lunch, he gave thanks and included a plea for God to watch over Anna. Details of his deep search on her parents troubled, intrigued, and confused him. Knowing her phone would be switched off, he left a message, telling her he'd be at her home when she arrived back with supper in hand and a lot of questions. Maybe her information would be more positive than what he had to share.

One last piece of research he wanted to conduct before he met with Anna was to refresh his memory about Germany during the time between the World Wars. Using a search engine few people knew about, Cullen found a wealth of information.

During the post-World War I years, German scientists escalated their activities in genetic research. Their interests included increase body strength, stamina, resistance to disease, and to prolong life. Several companies flourished under the radar. Allied countries knew nothing about them and the Weimar Republic Government officials probably didn't either. The Depression interfered and some companies faced financial ruin, while others merged.

He next discovered the unethical practices management at FARA used to benefit their organization. Accountants infiltrated other facilities, tampered with their books to bring about financial crises which then enabled FARA to purchase them at a low cost. No wonder they succeeded when many others failed, and since most of their activities were probably illegal, their competitors had no recourse with the authorities.

Further reading detailed Hitler's involvement. In the late 1930s after he became more powerful, he openly sanctioned genetic research, but in fact, he'd been an active proponent for years. Cullen stared off into the distance. History books documented what happened to thousands of prisoners at concentration camps prior to and during World War II. He couldn't help but wonder if FARA had been involved. Given their ruthless practices, he figured they were.

He opened another search engine to find out more about FAFA, his phone rang. William Blake.

After the greeting, William jumped right into his reason for calling. "Sylvia contacted me and she's extremely upset and nervous. A company official she's never met before, grilled her about Claire. Asked if she'd ever been to Claire's home. Did they socialize outside of the office? What did she know about Claire's family?" He huffed as if out of breath. "All Sylvia could say was she knew Claire had a daughter named Anna and that they'd met when she came to collect her mother's personal property."

"I don't mean to tarnish your daughter's ethics, but do you know if that's true?"

William hesitated. "She doesn't lie, but given the goings on at FARA, I'm not so sure. We're meeting after work this evening and I'll ask. See if she has any details to add."

"Good. Thank you for sharing. No wonder Sylvia is uncomfortable." Cullen concluded his notes. "Will she let me call her directly?"

"When I first asked, she agreed, but after today's development, she doesn't want you to contact her. Not even on her cell."

"I can understand her predicament." He contemplated telling William Anna started work at FARA today, but decided against it. "Anything else?"

"No, but I'll be in touch if Sylvia provides more information."

"Thanks. Every little bit, no matter how trivial, might help."

Cullen ended the call and rocked in his desk chair. Why was Sylvia questioned about Claire's family? Had someone discovered Anna Knight, new employee at FARA, was indeed her daughter? When he visited with Anna this evening, he'd try to convince her to quit. In the meantime, he continued his online research.

Delving deeper into old records and using a translation app, he discovered more about FARA. The company was founded in 1942 in Ulm, northwest of Munich, not 1969 in Seattle as stated on their website. Referring back to notes he took when Anna shared the contents of the documents from Claire's safe, he underlined Das Institut für Genforschung. Hugo and

Clara had signed contracts there in 1930 and 1934 respectively.

He was unable to link FARA with this institute, but he did locate a list of their board of directors and a Frank Ahn served as president. Cullen had no idea how common the last name was but since both Anna's parents worked for Frank Ahn Research Associates, the name seemed more than a coincidence. When Mr. Ahn left Das Institut, maybe Clara and Hugo, along with other scientists, joined him and formed the new research company.

Spurred on by this discovery, he continued and located a birth certificate for a Frank Ahn born in Leipzig, June, 1890. If he was the same guy, he'd have been 52 when he founded his company in Germany, but 79 when he established FARA in Seattle. At this point Cullen couldn't prove the two men were one and the same, or if they were father, son, grandson.

An article Cullen had read earlier in his research chugged through his memory. A Seattle newspaper published a piece about the new research facility. He located the article online and reread it. Yes. During the course of the interview, Frank revealed he was in his 50s. The accompanying photo showed a man who could have been that age and not 79.

Cullen checked his watch. Time to prepare a meal to take to Anna. Her instructional paperwork indicated she would be returned to her vehicle by five thirty. While waiting for the leftover salmon to thaw for a seafood salad, he conducted a quick search and located a Washington State death certificate for Frank Ahn, dated April, 2019. His research would be much more conclusive if these men had middle names. But if this guy was the same Frank Ahn, then he died at age 129, probably a recipient of his company's genetic manipulation.

Chapter 13

The padded chairs in the small orientation classroom were comfortable, but Anna shifted in her seat and flexed her fingers. She was not the only restless trainee. Raul leaned forward, then back, twirled his pen between his fingers until Judy glared at him. Again. He'd stuck by Anna's side like clingwrap ever since she'd clung to his arm after seeing her mother's portrait. She was pleased to note he had washed off his spicy aftershave. His behavior wasn't romantic. More like an overwhelmed teen seeking adult guidance.

During their many sessions, Judy seemed to single him out for criticism—when she wasn't scolding Anna for little to no experience in the scientific world. Raul's answers demonstrated his intelligence, but some of his questions and actions were impetuous.

The windowless walls of the classroom were festooned with a periodic chart—understandable considering the location—and colorful posters displaying human internal systems such as muscular, nervous, respiratory, and placement of organs. But no clock, and without her cell phone, Anna had no idea how much longer they'd be treated to Judy's droning voice.

Smiling, the instructor shoved her hands into her pockets. "That's all for today. I'll take you to your temporary lockers which already have your names listed. Deposit your notebooks and pens, and once in the foyer, the guard will return your personal items before you board the van. Let's go."

Judy led the way down a narrow hall to a bank of olive-green lockers, many with combination locks hanging on the open doors. Watching with a stern stare, she nodded as each trainee obeyed the command. "Good. Close the locks, and here are the combinations. Memorize yours, please." She handed out slips of paper. "Follow me."

They walked single file along more narrow maze-like halls that twisted and turned. Judy opened a security door with her badge and led them to the metal detector. After they were cleared, she approached the front desk. "Check that all your belongings are here. The van is parked out front. Hand your nametag to the driver when you reach your destination." Squinting at Raul, she added, "The van will leave at nine o'clock tomorrow morning. If you are not there, I will accept that as your resignation from the program." She pivoted and disappeared through the door.

Personal items in hand, the four trainees left the building and entered the van. Anna expected some conversation, especially from Raul, or even Natalie, but no one seemed inclined to chat. She figured if they, like her, where exhausted by the day of lectures, she couldn't blame them. Five more days. When would she get the opportunity to see more of the facility or meet other employees?

Knowing Cullen waited for her at home helped pass

the time in the van and later in her own car. She didn't have much to share with him, but hoped he had more to offer than just his support for her to continue with the training program.

Astride his motorbike, dressed in blue jeans and a sky-blue T-shirt, the sight of Cullen in her driveway took Anna's breath away. Corny to even think about, but she clutched the shirt over her heart to slow it's beating and drew in air. She parked alongside him, snagged her purse, and hurried to her front door before he noticed the blush she felt rise up her face.

She fumbled inserting the key, but eventually managed. "Come in. Thank you for bringing a meal. I'm starving. If left up to me, I'd heat a frozen meal." Jabbering as she set placemats, plates, and silverware on the dining table eased her embarrassment.

"No big deal. Seafood salad with homemade dressing." He removed a large bowl and a glass jar from his tote and placed them on the table. "Can I help with anything else?"

"Yeah. Iced water. I'll wash up and join you in a minute." She headed to her bedroom and closed the door. In the bathroom, she splashed water on her heated face, removed the band from her ponytail and brushed her hair. She inserted her contact lenses because her eyes were objecting to the glasses she'd worn all day and not because of Cullen's presence. Satisfied her heart and head were in sync for the encounter, she returned to the dining room. She and Cullen would be sharing important information for the next hour or two. Nothing more.

Cullen waited until she sat, then settled in the chair opposite, and bowed his head. "Thank you, Father, for keeping Anna safe today. Please help her search for answers. Nourish our mind and bodies with this food so we can serve You. In Jesus name. Amen." He opened the jar of dressing and passed the salad to her.

Whiffs of delicate salmon and tangy vinaigrette set her mouth to watering. The flavor matched the aroma. Yum.

Conversation touched on non-consequential topics while they ate, a deliberate choice on Anna's part, and maybe Cullen read her mood and contributed to the exchanges.

After she cleared away the dishes and returned to the table, Cullen removed a zippered case from his tote and withdrew a folder and notepad. "I have a lot to share with you, but first, I want to hear about your day."

"There's not much to tell." She described Judy and her fellow trainees.

Cullen jotted down details. "Do you think one might prove an ally?"

"Maybe Raul. I almost fainted when I saw Mother's portrait in the lobby. I grabbed his arm, and he might have misinterpreted my action. He almost never left my side."

"He could be useful."

"Our day was filled with lecture after lecture. On protocols, safety measures when using chemicals, methods to conduct experiments. As if we'd never been in a science class before. But I suppose necessary as a refresher. We had limited exposure to the facility. The same classroom, all day, narrow hallways with no signage. A huge cafeteria but we were shepherded in and out so fast I don't remember much about it, and then we ate our meal in a small side room. Tight security everywhere. A color-coded badge is necessary to open any door. I might not be able to discover much."

"A lot will depend on where you're assigned to work. You might have more flexibility the longer you are there."

Anna noted Cullen's solemn tone and the grim line of his mouth. "What's wrong? You don't sound convinced."

He opened the folder and tapped the papers inside. "I have a few more questions before I share the results of my extensive research. I know your training goes through Saturday. Did Judy give any indication as to what will be covered during the next few days?"

"A brief outline. Actual lab work, conducting prescribed experiments. More lectures spread out this week, and an exam on Friday. Can you believe it. Takes me back to university. The results will determine our field of concentration. You'd better believe I'm going to read up on genetics, and might contact my mentor, Dr. Faulkner."

"Is that wise?"

"I used him as a reference on my FARA application."

"Right."

"Since I haven't worked in the scientific arena, I need a crash course and he's the one to provide it. Besides, I'd be devastated if I flunked and was removed from the program." Anna tucked a strand of hair behind her ear. She had to pass the exam.

"Fair enough." Cullen stretched his legs under the table. "Ready for my data?"

She nodded.

"Many details jive with what we learned about your parents. Either they were named after ancestors or they were born a long time ago. I discovered a Frank Ahn was born in 1890, founded FARA in 1942, in Germany. I assume the facility survived the bombings during the war since it was located in Ulm, near Munich. He died in 2019, in Seattle. Either Frank from FARA was named after his ancestor, or he died at age 129 of organ failure."

The coincidental details swam around in Anna's mind. She blinked to settle the chaos. "Organ failure. Frank, my parents, many executives at FARA all dying from organ failure. They could have been subjects of their own experiments." She rose and paced to the front door and back.

"Exactly what I was thinking."

"We might have solved one of my mysteries. My parents lived a long time, worked in a lucrative business, and that's how they accumulated their wealth. Since Mother's portrait hangs in their research facility alongside Frank's must mean she played a big part in their success."

Cullen folded his arms across his broad chest.

Drawing her gaze from his perfect physique to his face, she noted his lips formed a thinner grim line than before. Back in her chair, she asked, "More information?"

"Yes, and it might be serious. I spoke with William today. Seems Sylvia has been subjected to questions about your mother." He looked Anna in the eye. "And her relationship to you."

"My mother, I understand. But why me?"

"That's what troubles me. I doubt anyone knows

Anna Knight, new FAFA recruit, is Claire's daughter, but they might find out, and then you—"

"Don't even suggest that I quit now."

"I think it best."

Head bowed, Anna swallowed the hash retort ready to fly out of her mouth. He had her welfare at heart, but how dare he tell her what to do? She looked straight ahead, avoiding his dark eyes. "I disagree. My quest is only half-fulfilled. Besides, if they find out Claire was my mother, what's the worst they can do? Fire me?"

Cullen shrugged. "If you won't follow my advice, then answer this question. What do you still hope to discover?"

Grasping her abdomen, her action blocked from his view by the table, she repeated what she'd said the previous day, "I need to know if the genetic modifications my parents received were passed on to me. Obviously, the changes were made before I was conceived. Will I outlive my peers? Will my children be affected? Do the adaptations carry over from generation to generation?" She blew out a breath and placed her hands on the table. "Those are the answers I crave."

He covered her hands with his.

The concern evidenced in his gesture helped eased Anna's troubled mind and softened her outrage. "I have to return."

"Okay. I'll support you although I disagree."

Removing her hands from his, Anna frowned. Sympathy from him one second, condescending tone the next. But she vowed to stick to her plan. "Since I can't take pictures or bring home any notes, I'll have to remember a lot of details."

"I'll work on that. Leave the logistics to me."

"You mean like a camera in the frame of my glasses?"

He laughed. "No. That's old school. I'll keep in mind you will pass through a metal detector to enter and exit the facility." The grin slipped from his face. "But I have a request. No, a demand. From now on, I will drop you off in the mornings and pick you up."

"That's possible until Saturday. After I'm vetted, I doubt you'd be allowed to drive to the facility. Remember, I told you what measures they took so we didn't know the location of the entrance."

"I'm sure you'll pass your exam. On Saturday you can ask Judy if your boyfriend can continue to transport you."

His reference to a beau warmed her heart. *If only.* But his insistence he accompany her still rankled. "I appreciate your concern, but is it necessary for you to take me each day?'

Again, he crossed his arms and stared at her. "Yes. I want FARA authorities to know someone has your back and will miss you if you disappear."

Anna stared at him wide-eyed as her mouth gaped.

Chapter 14

Cullen arrived at the rendezvous point minutes before the black van parked in the middle of the lot. The door opened and out stepped a tall woman. "Judy, I presume."

"Yup. Clipboard at the ready." Anna adjusted her glasses. "Do you want to meet her?"

"Not yet. At this stage, I want her to know I'm with you and I care."

"Your comment last night scared me. I—"

"It was meant to. Based on my research, FARA authorities have been ruthless in the past. I'm not going to give them the benefit of the doubt unless they earn it." Cullen checked his watch. "Nearly nine. Maybe the others don't want to continue."

"They have a few more minutes. I'd rather not go through the training by myself and be the only person subjected to Judy's disdain."

"You didn't mention any problems. What happened?"

Anna crossed and uncrossed her legs. "In between railing on Raul, she'd remind me that although I had the appropriate degrees, I had no experience in the scientific world."

"I have confidence you'll surprise her. Here comes a pickup. Raul?"

"No. Marcus. And that's Natalie in the sedan. I'm glad I won't be alone. But I wish Raul would make it. I imagine he'd be fun to work with. He's curious and speaks his mind. Oh, good. There he is."

"I'll be here by five fifteen. Remember, the security company is scheduled to install the system today at the Bainbridge house. I won't let that interfere with picking you up on time." Cullen opened his door and stepped out. He deliberately wore a well-fitting T-shirt, knowing it advertised his physical attributes. "Let me get your door then I'll walk with you to the van."

"Okay." Anna waited for him and climbed out of his Jeep while securing her hair in a ponytail.

He set his arm around her shoulders, and after an initial wince, she walked beside him as if they were a couple.

Tight-lipped Judy eyed their approach. Cullen contemplated how much he should act the part without adversely affecting Anna's success. He stopped a few feet from the van, bent and whispered in her ear. She turned her face upward, and he planted a kiss on her lips. She hid her surprise well, accepted her name tag from Judy, and entered the van. He knew he'd hear all about his action when he picked her up, but he felt the gesture suited the moment. And he'd enjoyed it too much for his composure. He returned to his vehicle and exhaled. *Watch it. Don't break your rule and get personally involved with a client.*

The van left promptly at nine. Cullen waited a few minutes before following it south on Highway 101. He recalled Anna saying the windows darkened about nine miles from Quilcene and checked his odometer. Other vehicles on the road helped make his pursuit less obvious. At least he hoped so. When the van turned right, Cullen noted the spot, and after he reached it, pulled to the shoulder, stopped, and took a photo for future reference. No signage, nothing to indicate a huge facility existed a few miles up the road. Or rather, dirt lane. It was well-traveled, but anyone passing would surmise it to be a driveway to a house.

Conscious of the time it would take to reach Anna's house, he headed to Bainbridge Island, arriving forty minutes later. Sam Redd, job supervisor from Hauser Security, texted him their arrival time. Cullen had half an hour to explore the opulent mansion.

At the top of the grand staircase, he stopped and surveyed the vast foyer and sitting area with its leather sofa and chairs, oriental rugs, and fancy carved furniture. No way could he envision Anna living here. Her rented house in Port Townsend suited her. Comfortable, minimally decorated, but with an artist's eye for subtlety. Nothing in this place looked like it belonged in her home. Cullen descended the stairs. Would being a millionaire change Anna? He doubted it.

The walls in the office hadn't been repaired yet. He'd check with Evan to see when the work would be done. At least the window in the garage had been replaced. Pillows and a blanket on a sofa in the living room indicated where Evan had spent each night. After the successful installation today, he could return home.

Cullen responded to the doorbell. Sam Redd was early. Two employees exited the Hauser pickup and stood behind Sam as he introduced himself.

They shook hands. "Come in. I'll be in the kitchen

if you need anything. How long will it take?"

Sam removed his cap and entered. "Considering the size of the house, probably three to four hours. Usually we work faster than that, but we're short on experienced techs." He indicated the workers behind him. "Trish has been with us a year, but Ken is a new hire."

Cullen nodded to both employees, and received a wide smile from petite, raven-haired Trish and a grunt from young and lean, Ken Fredrich.

"We'll get started, then. Let's get the supplies." Sam headed outside with his workers on his heels.

Cullen retreated to the kitchen table where he'd left his laptop, fingers itching to continue his research. "Lord, please help me find answers to Anna's questions so she can leave FARA."

Chapter 15

The pressure from Cullen's kiss lingered on Anna's lips long after the van stopped at FARA. She'd ignored disapproving glances from Judy and disappointed gazes from Raul during the ride.

Personal items deposited at the front desk, notepads and pens collected from their lockers, the four trainees had followed Judy to a different classroom which housed a lab at the rear.

Maybe her imagination ran wild, but throughout the morning's lecture and experiments, Anna was sure Judy singled her out for the most obscure questions. All because she had a beau or did the woman have another reason? Wilting under another reprimand for a failed experiment, Anna sank down to her stool and folded her arms.

Marcus smirked and muttered, "Anyone with a degree in biology should know that—"

"Enough, class." Judy stared at her students. "We all make mistakes. Now, clean up the lab before we go to lunch."

Unsure why Judy came to her defense, Anna meticulously completed her share of the task. On their way to the cafeteria, Raul, now free of the offending aftershave, slipped behind her and gently patted her shoulder. She smiled at him and mouthed, "Thanks."

Laden cafeteria trays in their hands, they were led by Judy to a rectangular table in the corner away from the others. "If you finish before I get back, please remain at the table."

Little conversation occurred while they ate, although Raul, seated beside Anna, tried to cheer her. "What work does your boyfriend do?" he whispered.

She remembered Cullen's advice to stick to the truth when possible. "He's a musician." Hoping to curtail Raul's interest, she added, "And a preacher."

The young man nodded, gulped down the last of his soda, and turned toward her. "He doesn't look like a preacher, but I suppose anyone can become a pastor." Raul placed his large hand on Anna's arm. "That didn't come out right. I mean..." He hung his head.

"Don't worry. First time I met him I was surprised to learn of his profession." Which was true in part.

Marcus shoved his half-full tray to the side and glared at Anna. "Do you believe in all that religious mumbo-jumbo? No wonder you're having such a hard time here." His characteristic smirk accompanied an eyeroll.

For the first time, Natalie entered the conversation. "Hey, guys, let's keep our opinions to ourselves and concentrate on the job. A good friend of mine works here. That's how I knew about the vacancies. She told me that seldom do all recruits in any intake make it. Odds are the person who makes the lowest grade on Friday's test will be axed."

Natalie's comments sobered the others. Anna rubbed her temples. At least now she didn't have to answer Marcus. Initially, her association with Cullen had increased her desire to commit her life to the Savior, but the very act of deliberately seeking employment at FARA was such a big lie that she doubted she could beg for God's forgiveness.

Judy arrived before anyone responded to Natalie. Anna tried to shake off her negative thoughts as the trainees carried their trays to the conveyer belt leading to the kitchen then traipsed behind Judy back to the classroom.

Lectures and conducting experiments continued for several hours. Anna had no more flubs and was pleased with her successes. The morning mistakes behind her, she actually looked forward to the next phase of training.

Judy settled on her high stool at the front of the classroom. "Get ready to take more notes." She waited until they were seated, then cleared her throat. "If hired, you will be research assistants. FARA conducts genetic research in many areas. You may move from one section to another as the need arises, therefore you have to be well-versed in many aspects of the business. Later this afternoon you'll be given a number of slides to view." She indicated state-of-the-art microscopes on the back counter. "This will be a refresher for some of you, but important, nonetheless."

Anna kept her head lowered, sure all eyes focused on her.

The instructor listed possible areas of concentration including therapeutics, gene expression analysis, and pathogen gene and genome sequencing.

All topics Anna had recently read about, but the one that interested her most was not mentioned. None of these methods would have added years to her parents' lives. She stared at her notebook and jabbed her pen at the words she'd written. How naive of her to expect Judy to discuss genetic modifications.

The door opened and a squat, balding man in a lime-green lab coat entered. Judy did a double take, hopped off her stool, and met him as he closed the door. He shielded his mouth with sheets of paper, and she bent to listen.

Judy shook her head. "I forgot."

"Do it now."

She accepted the paper from the man, ushered him out, and cleared her throat again. "Change of plans." Judy handed out the paper and returned to her stool. "It seems your application forms weren't complete. Please write your full name and the names of your parents. Where they live and their occupations."

A cold shiver flittered across Anna's shoulders and the familiar anxiety critters began stirring in her gut. Had FARA discovered she was Claire's daughter? Every strand of common sense urged Anna to object, but that would only draw attention.

Marcus, whom Anna assumed was a yes-man, raised his hand. "I don't see how this information is any of FARA's business. I have a high security clearance and—"

"No completed form, no job. It's that simple." Judy scowled. "Hurry up. I have more curriculum to cover this afternoon."

Lying was the only option available to Anna. Could she use Lexie's parents? They had taken her in as a second daughter. Pen poised over the blank page, Anna hesitated. Providing their details might put them at risk, and if FARA investigated, Anna would be fired.

Natalie and Raul appeared to be done. Anna had to think fast. What if she had no parents? Orphan. Foster care. Yes. She scribbled a brief life story. Her parents died when she was ten. She went from one foster family to another. Never adopted. Can't remember names, locations. Too traumatic. And it all happened in...Tennessee. Satisfied the information would make it harder for anyone to track her past, she folded the piece of paper and handed it to Judy who gathered all the pages. In a moment of indecision and confusion, Anna opened her mouth to ask for her paper back then snapped it shut. She needed to keep her identity a secret. For now.

As instructed earlier in the day, Judy presented the trainees with a number of slides which they studied under the powerful microscopes. Refresher course for sure. It had been years since Anna had viewed cells, chromosomes, plasma. Identifying labels were included with each slide, but Judy reminded the pupils that on the exam, they would have to provide the details. Anna's heart sank. Scanning articles online helped educate her on the subject. Now she had to include sites that provided in-depth molecular study. Would she ever have time to sleep?

Judy interrupted the class. "That's all we have time for today. Replace the slides in the cases. You're in for a treat. We're going to tour parts of the facility." She beamed as she opened a tote bag and withdrew orange clothing. "Put on these lab coats and replace your nametag onto the lapel."

The color of the coats reminded Anna of prison jumpsuits. They certainly would be easy to spot as the trainees ventured beyond the bland classroom and halls.

"Our first stop will be your lockers. Deposit your notebooks and pens."

Once they completed that task, Judy walked swiftly ahead of her students down the hall and through security to the foyer. She stood beside the counter and pointed to the huge portraits. "I'm sure you've read about FARA's history on our website. Here is our founder, Frank Ahn."

Raul, head and shoulders above the others, asked, "Who is Clara Schneider?"

Slinking behind Raul, Anna hung her head, glad she'd hidden the white streak in her hair as Clara's was very evident.

"Clara worked here for a long time."

Anna almost choked but hid her reaction with a cough.

Judy continued, "She was influential in basic research and pioneered many successful procedures we use today."

"Are they both deceased?" Marcus asked.

"Um, yes."

"What are some of the procedures Ms. Schneider introduced?"

"Good question, Marcus. I like your enthusiasm. She discovered many genes that can be manipulated and...you'll learn more later on." Judy flushed. "We need to keep to the schedule. This way, please." She pivoted and headed back to the security door.

Anna took one last look at her mother, then hurried to catch up to the others. Judy almost gave away a secret. Maybe she would be a source Anna could probe if hired.

The tour took them to several windowless labs where they observed the proceedings from the door or a viewing platform. All highly sophisticated. Judy provided superficial explanations while preening. Obviously, proud of the company and its mission.

Next, she stopped at an elevator and turned to address her audience. "As you can see, entry to this or any elevator, requires a special color-coded badge. You may be required to navigate on your own, but for the most part, you will always be accompanied by a senior employee. Your official badges will inform you which labs or elevators you can access." She flashed her badge at a pad on the wall. "This will be our last stop for today."

While waiting for the elevator, Anna mentally paired activities seen in each lab with the color coats the scientists wore. Information which might prove invaluable in the future. The door opened and they stepped inside. There were no buttons on a panel as seen in regular conveyances. Instead, the same type of pad she'd seen beside the door was mounted where the control buttons should have been.

Again, Judy flashed her badge and lighted yellow numerals appeared on the pad. In quick succession, she punched six—if Anna counted correctly—and the elevator began to move. Not upward, as she predicted, but down. Down, down. There was no display indicating the floors they passed, but it seemed as if they were well below ground level.

When the door opened, Judy took a few steps then stopped. "Please stay close together. The lab we're going to is at the end of this hall." She turned and walked briskly along the narrow passage.

The air temperature dropped noticeably, and a faint odor of week-old socks wafted past Anna, transporting her at once to high school science labs. She covered her nose with her hand, but soon ignored the smell.

Judy held her badge ready to swipe on the pad beside a door. "This is our—"

"Ms. Coates, what are you doing on this floor with your trainees?"

The gruff voice halted Judy's action. She dropped her arm, spun around, face ashen. "Um, Doctor Mueller, I want to show them our cancer research department."

"Not on the plan. Get them out of here immediately and see me in my office after they leave the facility." The elderly man stormed down the hall in the opposite direction.

Oops.

Without a word or any reaction, Judy led her students back the way they'd come. In the foyer, she pointed to the security guard behind the counter. "Leave your lab coats here, then collect your items, and don't be late tomorrow." She disappeared through a door she hadn't used previously.

On board the van, aware the driver might be listening to their conversation although the dividing panel had been lowered, Anna kept her voice low and leaned toward Raul. "What do you make of our instructor's mistake today?"

He frowned. "Not sure. I think she was trying to instill in us how fortunate we should feel if hired."

"I agree." Natalie swung her legs around and joined the conversation. "My friend told me that although FARA is a prestigious research facility, they are short-staffed. Personally, I will be honored to work there."

Short-staffed because so many seasoned scientists have died. Anna barely had time to complete her thought when Marcus turned to face Natalie.

"You're not the only person with connections. A former professor of mine works at FARA and we keep in touch regularly. He knows Judy and said she has a questionable past."

Anna's antennae perked up. "Like what?"

Pleased with the attention, Marcus actually smiled. "Well, for one, she has an American accent, but she was born in Germany."

"And how is that questionable?" Natalie glared at Marcus.

"If you take that attitude with me, I won't tell you anything else."

"Hold on, Marcus." Anna reached across the aisle but dropped her hand when he shrank back. "We...I want to know more. Please, continue."

He waited a few seconds. "Okay. Judy Coates is not her real name."

Now, we're getting somewhere. Anna refrained from probing and hid her interest by focusing on her shoes.

"What is her name?" Raul asked.

Huffing out a contented sigh, Marcus folded his arms across his bony chest. "Frida Dietrich."

"Come on, you guys." Natalie tsk-tsked. "So what if Judy doesn't have a German accent. Maybe she came to America as a child. And lots of people change their names, for many reasons."

Marcus pursed his lips. "I think it's noteworthy is all. And there's more."

Not wanting to show too much interest, Anna bit her tongue and mentally repeated the name Frida Dietrich over and over

But then Raul chimed in. "Out with it, Marcus. You know you're dying to tell us."

"My professor said Judy is high up in the managerial hierarchy, but—"

"I think Dr. Mueller might disagree."

"Raul, quit interrupting me."

"I don't care about that. Why did we have to provide our parents' names and occupations? That was strange. You even complained."

The dividing panel behind the driver raised and the windows returned to clear, curtailing any further discussion. Natalie straightened, Raul and Marcus stared at the countryside flashing past, and Anna cradled her face in her hands. Questionable past, indeed. More research for Cullen.

Chapter 16

Due to the size of Anna's house on Bainbridge Island, the Hauser Company spent most of the day installing security monitors on all the windows and doors, three control panels and motion sensitive cameras inside, and MS lighting outside. Sam apologized for the lengthy installation, blaming faulty sensors and inexperienced help.

Cullen arrived at Anna's pick-up location just after five. He sat on the hood of his Jeep and waited.

The black van parked in its usual spot. The four trainees alighted, and Marcus stormed off to his truck, but Cullen's gaze followed Anna. Her hair was free of its ponytail and the breeze blew strands across her face. When she drew closer, he noted the dark circles under her eyes and her drooping shoulders.

He opened her door and she slumped into the seat. Sure she was not in the mood to keep up the boyfriend charade, he resisted giving her a hello kiss. "You look tired."

"I am. Did you prepare a meal again? I have a lot to share, but no energy to cook."

He climbed in and buckled his seatbelt. "The security company took longer than I expected. Call

Tom's restaurant and order meals to go."

"Good idea." She extracted her phone from the purse she'd left in his vehicle and placed an order.

"Do you want to talk now or wait until later?"

"Now. I'm bursting with info." She related a couple of events from her day.

"I'll check on Frida Dietrich. But what concerns me most is Judy asking for your parents' details. Combine that with someone questioning Sylvia about your mother, and my caution alarm rings loud. Raised in foster care. Quick thinking. That will thwart any search for a while. Why do you think she asked for those details?"

"What if FARA is trying to locate children born to people who underwent genetic modifications?"

"But if they've been conducting these experiments for a long time, surely they've had the opportunity to study offspring already?"

"It depends when the subjects underwent the treatment. Consider my folks. Unless proven otherwise, I'm assuming the Hugo and Clara named in the documents we found are in fact my parents. Mother would have been, um, eighty-eight at my birth." Anna blew out a breath. "Saying the age out loud makes me doubt my supposition."

"It's mind-boggling." Cullen stopped outside Vaughn's Vittles. "I'll get our food and we can continue this discussion after we've eaten."

Cullen paid for the order, had a brief chat with Tom and Lexie, then hurried back to his vehicle. He handed Anna the to-go bag and savory aromas of roasted vegetables filled the car. "Lexie wants you to call her."

"I've been busy studying in the evenings and

haven't made time to do anything else. I'll talk with her tonight."

A few minutes later, he pulled into Anna's short driveway.

She unlocked the front door and dumped her purse on the sofa. "Would you mind setting the table while I freshen up."

"Sure, but before you go, please get me a notepad and pencil."

She rummaged through items on her desk in the corner and produced a yellow legal pad and pencil.

Cullen located silverware and set out their salads and sandwiches on the table, together with two glasses of iced water. Then he proceeded to create a timeline for Anna's parents. He didn't have their birthdates memorized, but he noted the dates of Claire's passing and Anna's birth.

She returned, her face freshly washed, no glasses, and her hair loose. "I'm glad I only ordered half a sandwich. I'm not hungry."

"Speak for yourself. I didn't find much I wanted to consume at your Bainbridge house." He chuckled. "That reminds me." He withdrew a business card from his pocket. "This is the company which installed your security system. I wrote the code on the back. The owner's manual is at the house. I gave Hauser my name and phone number for the monitoring office to call if there's a breach. It doesn't make any sense for you to be contacted if you're at FARA without your phone. I signed you up for the deluxe package. If the alarm is triggered, a security guard will be notified of the location of the breach and will check the perimeter, or enter the house if necessary."

"Thanks. I'll give Bonnie the code. She's scheduled to visit the house twice a week." Anna sipped her water. "By the way, her young granddaughter's fractured arm is healing well."

Cullen poured vinaigrette dressing over his salad. "Glad to hear that. However, I don't think it's wise to give her the code."

"Why?" Anna frowned. "Ahh. You think I should dispense with her services so fewer people know the code."

"Yes. At least while you're at FARA."

"Okay, but I will tell her about the alarm system. And of course, I'll pay her. Then when I'm ready to sell the place, she can do a thorough clean and help me prepare for an estate sale."

"You can afford to hire someone to—"

"Don't talk about money." Anna thumped the table. "Their money."

Cullen wanted to complete his timeline while they ate, but obviously Anna needed time to relax before he confronted her with the seriousness of her working at FARA.

"Sorry." He gently took her hand and held it. "Father, thank You for all our blessings, especially this food. We are in constant need of Your comfort. Please wrap Your arms around Anna and ease her concerns. In Jesus's name. Amen."

She smiled and took a deep breath as he released her hand. "Your prayers are always succinct. Thank you for reminding me of God's power."

At the conclusion of the meal during which they'd spoken little, Cullen cleared the table, ignoring Anna's protest. He showed her the timeline he'd compiled.

"Before you continue with your day's events, help me fill in more dates."

"With the assumption that Hugo and Clara are indeed Hugh and Claire?"

"Right."

"The documents indicate Clara was born October, 1907, and Hugo December, 1901. Their marriage certificate is dated January 11, 1930. All in Germany. I have their parents' names from the birth records." She fetched a slip of paper from her desk and handed it to him.

"Thanks. Remind me when they signed their contracts with that German institute."

"Hugo in 1930 and Clara in 1934."

He added all the new details. "You also have a date for the marriage of modern-day Hugh and Claire."

"January 11, 1990. Oh, and my father died in 2001. I've ordered a copy of his death certificate. I see you have the date of Mother's passing, and the year of my birth."

"One more question. Does that marriage certificate indicate how old they were at the time?"

"No."

After he included the date of her father's death, she ran her finger along the line from her parents' marriage in 1930 to her birth. "If they had any children during these years, they'd be in their eighties now."

Rubbing his chin, he leaned back. "This all seems like the plot to a cheesy Sci-Fi movie."

"Siblings fifty or sixty years older than me." Anna fanned her face with the pad. "I'm overwhelmed and..." She began to giggle while breathing hard and almost choked.

Concerned, Cullen scooted closer. "You'd better calm down before you hyperventilate. Do you need a drink?"

She shook her head.

"Do you want me to leave so you can rest?"

"I'm okay." She sucked in a few breaths and straightened her shoulders. "I can't rest until we explore this absurd reality that is probably mine."

He looked at her facial expression. Determination had replaced panic. "Back to that reality, then." It was his turn to trace the timeline. "Your parents could have undergone their genetic modifications anytime while employed in Germany or here in Seattle."

"I have a different idea. Let me think out loud. As far as we know the genetic manipulations were to prolong life, increase stamina, etcetera, not to reverse the aging process, only to delay it." She rested her elbows on the table and stared at him. "Mother never seemed to age normally in the photos I have of her. Hold on a sec." She ran back to another part of the house and returned with two picture frames which she set on the table.

"Your mother was a beautiful woman."

"Don't get distracted. Look at this one." Anna pointed to an eight by ten frame of Claire holding a baby while standing in the living room of the Bainbridge house. "Mother said this was taken when I was six months old." She sat and moved a smaller frame closer. "And this one was taken when Lexie and I opened our art institute, three years ago. Mother condescended and came to our celebration. Twenty-four years apart. Does it look like she aged one bit?"

He picked up the smaller photo and studied it. "Not

at all."

"Mother looks about thirty at the most in the first photo. Therefore, I think she underwent the modifications when she was that age." Anna nabbed the pencil and marked on the timeline when Clara would have been in her thirties. "Anywhere in the late 1930s or early 1940s." She folded her arms.

"That makes sense, in this strange world we're describing."

Nodding toward the picture of her mother, Anna frowned. "Images of the last two times I saw mother just flashed across my mind. Both times—once at her home and then in the hospital—the rooms were darkened. She said the light hurt her eyes. Her hair was loose, and she wore no makeup." Anna twirled a strand of her hair. "Even in the muted light, Mother looked much older, which at the time seemed normal. But now when I compare the photo to my last image of her, it's almost as if whatever had been done to her genes was breaking down or being rejected by her body."

"Maybe that's what happened to all the FARA people who've died recently."

"I'd bet on it." She pointed to the mantel. "That's the only photo I have of Papa, and he looks to be in his fifties. I wonder if he agreed to the treatment first, then when Mother underwent the modifications, the scientists had advanced the process. Papa died twenty-one years before Mother, but chronologically, he was six years older."

Cullen's gaze focused on Claire's pictures, then Hugh's, and finally on the timeline. "I have a slew of ideas bouncing on a trampoline in my brain. Hear me out." He extracted the list of names he'd found in

Claire's condo from his wallet, turned to a clean page on the pad, and wrote as he talked. "William Blake confirmed seven of these were FARA employees who died recently. I'll check to see if any of them worked with your folks at Das Institut." He held up his hand to Anna when she attempted to speak. "I understand they might have changed their names, too. But it's worth a try. Frida Dietrich is already on my list to investigate." Grasping her hand, he asked, "Do you want me to track down any siblings you might have?"

Surprised by the fierce expression on her face and by the force with which Anna yanked her hand free and stood, Cullen rose, too, and drew her into a hug. The action could have backfired if her anger hadn't dissipated.

She melted against his chest and muttered, "No. I…I can't deal with that right now." Pushing away, she looked up at him.

The tears pooling in her eyes nearly broke his heart. "Anna, I think you shouldn't—" She stiffened, and he changed tactics. "Let's sit and think rationally. Okay?"

To answer, she turned and plopped onto the sofa.

He sat beside her and held back his words until her breathing returned to normal. "I can see the toll this venture has taken on you these past two days."

The few seconds of silence warned him he'd crossed the line anyway.

"I admit I'm tired and feeling the pressure of succeeding. I have to pass the test on Friday, so I'm studying at night. Reading everything on gene therapy I can access online." She folded her arms again.

"I'm aware of that. But what about the emotional toll? Are you prepared to handle what you might discover?"

"I can't answer that since I don't know what I'll discover." She pushed up and strode to the mantel. "But I'll tell you this. I'm not quitting. I will find out why the portrait of Clara Schneider or Claire Taylor hangs in FARA's research facility. And why she never seemed to age."

"I understand."

"How can you? I've mentioned this before. There's a great possibility that my genes have been altered. Were already when I was conceived. I have to know if I'll have a normal lifespan, or am I a freak? Will I outlive a husband? Will my children be freaks, too?"

He had no ready answer and held his peace.

"During the past week, you've learned a lot about my past, but you don't know *me*." She prodded her chest. "So back off. Thanks for all your help. Send your bill to Mr. Jennings and close the door on your way out." Face red, she stormed from the room.

Cullen had never been fired by a client. He'd had a few who changed their minds and paid him what they owed. Not sure what to do next, he stood and looked around the room. He wasn't about to leave with so much unfinished business. Dare he follow Anna?

Footsteps echoed in the hall. She reappeared in the living room, fists on her hips. "You're still here."

"I...can't leave yet." He held out his hands as if to ward off the anger emitting from her stoic body language. "Please listen to my suggestions, and then I'll go."

Chin up, she gave her head an imperceptible toss. "Be quick. I have a lot of work to do."

"Since you're determined to return to FARA, please

consider befriending Natalie and Marcus so you can make use of their contacts already working there. They might be beneficial resources. Keep in mind the safety hints we already discussed. And don't shut me out. I want to help."

"I'll keep you informed." She pivoted and took two steps then turned. "I'm sorry I yelled at you, but even though you worded your ideas carefully, you want me to quit, and you have no right to tell me what to do."

"Okay, but I can care about your welfare, can't I?" Cullen almost regretted his words, but was rewarded with the positive change in Anna's demeaner.

Her shoulders lost their rigidness and she walked toward him, stopping at the table. "The research you've done and the documents we found all point to a questionable past for me. One minute, I dwell on the possibility my parents were born at the beginning of the 1900s. The next, I return to reality and are certain they were born twenty, thirty years before I was. The first assumption is so improbable. Fantasy. A nightmare, even."

"That much I get."

"I really do appreciate your help and concern for me, but I must decide which reality to accept. If modern-day Claire and Hugh were never subjected to genetic modifications then I can go about my business and put Mother's money to good use. But," she sank into a chair at the table, "the gnawing knots in my gut tell me this second assumption is not true."

"I agree. We know too much about FARA's nefarious actions in the past and their bogus website." He joined her at the table, hoping the rip in their relationship could be mended. "Hey, I have an idea.

There are many research facilities. Could you go to one and have them, I don't know what the technical term is, test your genes to see if they are what you call normal?"

She reared back and laughed, but the sound held little humor. "No, I can't do that. First of all, I haven't studied the process to know if they can even tell since my genes have always been this way. And I certainly don't want to advertise the fact I think they've been altered and risk being labeled a lunatic."

"Of course. That was a dumb recommendation."

"I could tell FARA who I really am. If my parents—the old parents or the modern-day set—did undergo genetic modifications, they would know."

It was Cullen's turn to rise from his seat with force. "You can't be serious. How can you trust FARA with your life when we know about their past?"

Face pale and a deep frown creasing her forehead, she looked at him with dread in her eyes. "What…what if my genes were altered when I was a child? I haven't considered that until now."

"Oh, Anna, please don't go back to FARA." He had no idea how to help alleviate her fear except to encourage her to give up on her quest.

She eased out of her chair, stepped to the front door and opened it. "I'll make a decision that I feel is best for my life. And I'll drive myself to the facility tomorrow. Goodnight."

Notepad tucked under his arm, Cullen walked out, words and thoughts unsaid. She was determined to continue with the training, and he had to find a way to stop her. On the ride home, he did think of one positive scenario. Maybe Anna would fail the test on Friday and not be offered a permanent job. As soon as the idea raised its head, he regretted it. She would be devastated if she failed, and he wouldn't be welcomed to comfort her.

Although exhausted, Cullen did not go to bed. After typing up notes and doing a load of laundry, he lay on his extra-long couch, eyes wide open while conflicting thoughts vied for consideration. Should he take Anna at her word and end the contract, or would she feel differently in the morning? He sat upright and slid his legs to the floor. She adamantly declared she wouldn't quit. Well, neither would he. He could research the topics he'd mentioned earlier, and keep watch over her from—

His phone buzzed. The security monitoring center informed him someone tried to jimmy open a window at Anna's house on Bainbridge Island. Helmet and keys in hand, Cullen dashed outside and climbed onto his Harley.

Chapter 17

The last website scoured for anything genetics related, Anna closed her laptop and rested her head on her pillows. During her hours of study, she'd been interrupted more than once by her conscience. She regretted her outburst toward Cullen. How could she expect him to understand her daunting problem—were her genes modified or not? But he'd been helpful and thoughtful, and when she remembered the hurt in his eyes, she wanted to scream.

Too tired to analyze her emotions, she showered and went to bed. The next morning while disguising the white streak in her hair, she decided to tell FARA about her parents, a sure way to obtain answers to the questions eating away at her. Staring at her refection in the bathroom mirror, she rolled her eyes. Yes. A complete one-eighty from yesterday, but she had to know. Satisfied with her decision, she drove to the Ride Share lot near Uncas, only to find Cullen sitting astride his motorbike.

Although the van waited with doors open, she walked calmly toward him and schooled herself to keep her voice even. But her anger at his presence surrendered to her heart which flop-flopped as she drew nearer. "Why are you here?"

"I figured you might not answer if I phoned, so I had to come. Someone tried to break into your Bainbridge house early this morning."

Muscles in her stomach knotted and her knees refused to hold her up. "What?" She grabbed the handlebars of his bike.

"I visited the house as soon as the monitoring company contacted me. They said no inside cameras were triggered, and the security guard confirmed all doors and windows were secure. He showed me pry marks on a kitchen window, and we concluded probably the alarm scared off the intruder. The attempt means someone is still determined to search your mother's house in spite of all the signage Hauser has displayed on the property." Cullen shrugged. "I stayed until time for me to come here, but I can't spend every night there and neither can Evan. I think we should consider hiring a guard or guards to keep watch, day and night."

Although processing the information he'd shared, Anna noted his use of the word *we* and turned her head so he wouldn't see her smile. Yeah, she needed him, in more ways than one.

"Thank you. I'm sorry for my unwarranted outbursts last night. Please don't close out my contract. I...want your help. As you said, the attempted break-in is disconcerting, and I agree to hire people to stay at the house." She glanced toward the van as Natalie boarded. "I have to go. Please come by this evening and I promise to listen to your advice, but I don't think I'll change my mind because I *will* pass the test."

He beamed at her, and she almost climbed on the

back of his bike.

"See you then, and I'll bring food, but I can't stay long. Bible study at seven, remember."

Scolding herself mentally, Anna hurried to the van in case she reneged on her decision. She would tell Judy today, but wasn't yet sure if she'd inform Cullen of her action.

The trainees kept up a steady flow of conversation until the van arrived at the facility. Anna shared little of importance, but was pleased to see Marcus opening up more instead of huddling against the window like a scared bird being shoved out of its nest.

As usual, the four students left their personal belongings at the counter and were escorted to their lockers where Judy awaited. Her usual sour expression seemed more acidic today.

"Good morning. Your orange coats are in your lockers. Bring them, please. We have a variety of labs to visit interspersed with instruction. Follow me."

She preceded the group down the hall to their classroom. As they entered, Anna hesitated beside the desk. Noting Judy's scowl, she changed her mind. Informing the instructor of her real parentage could wait another day. Or two. Once seated, notebook at the ready, Anna lowered her chin. No one from her past could have accused her of being wishy-washy, that is, from her normal life, but her circumstances now were as far from normal as the moon from the earth.

A knock at the door, and a middle-aged man in an electric wheelchair entered. Using his left hand, he manipulated the controls, the chair turned, and he faced the group. His navy-blue lab coat set off his sparse rust-colored hair. Green eyes sparkled as he surveyed the trainees. His gaze rested on Anna, and she couldn't help but smile. Unless he hid his disdain well, he appeared pleased to be in their company.

"Students, this is Dr. Victor Hays. He will be your instructor today and tomorrow." Judy nodded then strode from the room and closed the door.

"Good morning. It's good to see your fresh, young faces. I hope you are prepared for a full day. We're going to delve into genetic research in depth. Of course, I won't divulge any facility secrets, but you need to be aware of all the good work we do here. If offered a job, you will play an integral part in our daily business." Dr. Hays opened the laptop set up on a tray across his knees. "Take notes if you must, but at the end of the day tomorrow, I'll have handouts ready."

Raul closed his notebook and leaned back. Anna kept her pen in hand, as did Natalie and Marcus.

"Our focus today will be on the characteristics of genes, their structure, and function." The teacher pointed to Raul, who quickly straightened. "Young man, dim the lights, please."

When Raul returned to his seat, he opened his notebook and grinned at Anna who was still absorbing the topic of the lecture. Genes. Genetic research. The reason she hoped to work at FARA. On full alert, she scooted to the edge of her chair.

Colorful strands of DNA swirled across the screen up front. Dr. Hays tapped computer keys, and one strand emerged, front and center. "We'll begin with the basics. Forgive me if this is old territory for some of you, but it's part of the curriculum. There are four types of genes. Who can name them?"

Ever the know-it-all, Marcus raised his hand.

"No need for such formality. Holler out your answer."

"Adenine, Thyine, Cytosine, and Guanine."

"Excellent."

Marcus hunched his shoulders and clasped his hands to his chest, obviously reveling in the praise. Judy never uttered such words.

A single strand of DNA dividing into four colors dominated the screen. "A gene is a section of DNA made up of sequences of *As, Cs, Ts,* and *Gs.* Each one is so tiny that twenty thousand of them are in every cell of our bodies." Dr. Hays went on to explain the function of each type of gene. He asked many questions and Marcus always seemed to blurt out the answer before anyone else. Most of his answers were correct, and his demeanor changed with each positive response. Head held high, shoulders back, and a grin to rival any cat, Cheshire or not.

He was almost unbearable smug during lunch. For once, they weren't closely monitored, but their bright orange coats labeled them as trainees.

Anna had forgotten to select a drink and halfway through her meal of beef lasagna—Judy was right, the cafeteria served excellent food—returned to the service line. While waiting to fill her cup with ice, she overheard two staff members speaking in German. The man and women wore navy-blue coats, which Anna surmised indicated employees of prominence at FARA, since Judy, Dr. Hays, and Dr. Mueller all wore them. Ears attuned to their words, Anna deliberately dropped a napkin to prolong her time at the ice machine. At first, they discussed a party they attended the previous evening, and then the man asked after Dr. Hays. The women replied his condition had improved and he was scheduled for a another intervention later that day. Man: Does his wife know yet? Woman: No. They will only inform Erica if it's a success. The employees turned away, out of earshot.

Erica Hays from the HR department? Anna filled her cup with ice and water and rejoined the group, however, she couldn't focus on her meal or the lively conversation. Back in the classroom, she paid close attention to Dr. Hays. His legs and right arm seemed to be paralyzed, but he could move his torso. So probably not a spinal injury. He would be their instructor again tomorrow. Would she see any change in his physical condition after another 'treatment'?

Afternoon lectures and videos provided more in-depth knowledge on gene therapy for patients with rare genetic disorders, gene patenting, and gene editing procedures. Anna had read about several of these topics, but Dr. Hays ended his discourse with a statement that set the cogs in her brain turning.

"We carry more of our mother's genes than our father's."

What would that bode for her future? Mother's gene manipulations seemed to last longer than Papa's.

Toward the end of the day, Dr. Hays escorted the trainees to the underground labs. They stopped at a door labeled *Stem Cell*, and he said in a hushed voice, "We are proud of our work in this area. Although stem cell research began over fifty years ago, the scientific community is making new discoveries almost daily. FARA is a leader in the field." He knocked on an opaque window beside the door, and seconds later, the glass cleared. "Step closer to observe, and if you have any comments, please lower your voice."

Several people in navy-blue coats peered at objects through fancy microscopes or buzzed about the room. Anna noted the lab coat colors the other scientists wore which matched the list on the door's access panel.

"Is it possible one of us might be assigned to this lab?" Marcus asked.

Dr. Hays nodded. "Let's move on." He maneuvered his chair down the hall to another lab and pointed to the sign on the door. "Epigenetics. What do you know about this subject?"

Anna shrugged and looked at her peers, fully expecting Marcus to answer.

But Raul shoved his hands onto his hips. "Epigenetics is a relatively new scientific area which studies how our behavior and environment can cause changes that affect the way our genes work." He grinned. "Something like that. I read about it last night."

"Good for you." Dr. Hays knocked on the window beside the door and as before, the glass cleared. He watched his colleagues for a few seconds. "Epigenetics is the study of heritable changes caused by the activation or deactivation of genes without any change to the underlying DNA sequence. And before you ask, no, you will not be assigned to this lab. I want you to know that FARA is at the forefront of all kinds of scientific research, especially genetics."

Music to Anna's ears. Did her parents experience these changes? A jillion other questions rambled through her mind, but Dr. Hays moved down the hall again and motored past two more labs, neither of which displayed any signs although they did have color-coded panels and opaque windows beside the doors.

Remembering Cullen's advice to keep a low profile, Anna clamped her mouth shut, sure one of the other students would ask the obvious question.

Natalie leaned toward Dr. Hays. "What kind of labs are these?"

"They're not in use at the moment." He maneuvered down the hall and turned left at the corner.

Last in line, Anna followed the others but slowed when she heard a door open behind her. Two employees in the popular navy-blue lab coats exited one of the *unused* labs and entered the other. Certain they were the same people she'd overheard in the cafeteria, Anna hurried to catch up with her peers. So much for Dr. Hays's honesty.

Chapter 18

During the return trip to Uncas, the four trainees kept up a lively discussion about all Dr. Hays had shared and shown them. Anna didn't reveal her sighting of staff at the supposed unused labs as her mind had automatically raced to her problem. Is that where FARA conducted genetic research that fell outside the medical community's accepted purview?

Marcus, probably the smartest of the group, contributed his fair share to the conversation. His interactions with Dr. Hays seemed to have drawn him out of his introvert persona. Anna even concluded he was someone she'd like to get to know outside of the job.

She called Cullen as soon as she retrieved her phone from the glovebox in her car, but her call went to voicemail. During the ten-minute drive home, she sorted through the day's events and decided which she needed to share with Cullen. As she pulled into her empty driveway, her heart sank. No motorbike. No Cullen. An insulated bag with a note taped to the lid awaited her at the front door.

Sorry I can't share the meal with you. I had an emergency situation with

*another client, and I need to prepare
for tonight's Bible study. I'll call you later.
Enjoy. CK*

Anna carried the bag inside and set it on the kitchen counter. Disappointment saturated her mind and body. She slouched and headed to the bathroom, washed her face, let her hair loose, and put in her contacts. *Dismiss Cullen's help one minute, yearn for his company the next. Annika Louis, make up your mind.*

Back in the kitchen, she opened the bag. Cullen had prepared lasagna. Anna laughed until tears wetted her cheeks. Oh, well. The same meal for lunch and supper. Why not? Although the cafeteria's dish rated five stars, Cullen's vegetarian version surpassed it, and probably contained far fewer calories. His unique salad dressing added to the experience.

Anna washed and dried Cullen's plate and bowl and set them on the counter beside his bag. She could take them to his house, but decided against a visit and returned to her chair at the table. Accustomed to a full social calendar of theater visits, musical performances, and activities in Port Townsend's vibrant art scene, late nights were part of Anna's life, but studying into the wee hours and days crammed with academics were taking a toll. She folded her arms on the table and rested her head on them. Thirty minutes later, she awoke with a start.

"You need a change of scenery." Anna seldom spoke her thoughts out loud, but this time, she heeded her advice. She had just enough time to shower and dress for an evening in Lexie's company, surrounded by people who believed in the God who created all their genes. The fact Cullen would be presenting the Bible lesson had nothing to do with her decision.

Seated beside Lexie, listening to the group sing Cullen's latest worship song, Anna drew in a deep breath and closed her eyes. She had to admit she'd paid little heed to the nudging of her spirit these past few days. In her quest to discover her mother's secret, she'd allowed the scientific world to overshadow her fledgling faith. She opened her eyes, grasped Lexie's hand and whispered, "Please pray for me."

Lexie squeezed her hand and nodded. No more words necessary. Her friend always knew exactly what she needed.

Setting his guitar beside his chair, Cullen said, "Tonight, I will conclude my three-part lesson on forgiveness by focusing on God's grace. I don't usually do this, but I have a handout which lists points we covered previously, as well as numerous Scriptures that remind us to forgive each other—and ourselves—as God has forgiven us. I included the points I want to emphasize about grace. If you'd like a copy, Tom will pass them out."

Anna accepted a page and followed along as Cullen highlighted major points. She was especially interested in his explanation of God's grace, defined as 'unmerited favor which rescues us from what justice demands'.

"We can't earn grace, we can't buy grace. One of the statements Paul makes in Ephesians 2:8 is that grace is a gift from God. But, as with any gift, it has to be accepted. God's grace is available to all who believe and repent. Reach for it, accept it, then live like you have it. Grace." Cullen rested his elbows on his knees.

"As humans, it's difficult for us to understand God's grace. We expect justice, but Christ died on the cross and paid the price to set us free."

Tom led a prayer and then people chatted or exited through the gate to the parking area. Anna folded the sheet of paper and slipped it into her purse for later referral. Not only did she need Cullen's review on forgiveness, but she was intrigued by the concept of grace.

"You look tired, ladybug." Lexie stood and set her hands on her hips. "Are you sure this gig is right for you?"

"Yes. I have to follow it through. If I pass the test on Friday, I want to work at FARA long enough to resolve my parental issues."

"I can't assume to understand, but I'll keep praying for you. We're short-staffed and Tom needs my help in the kitchen. Call more often." Lexie patted Anna's shoulder then pivoted and entered the restaurant.

Still seated, Anna placed a hand over her middle when Cullen sat beside her. Her motion did nothing to calm the flutter of wings.

"Sorry I couldn't join you for supper."

"No problem. I enjoyed the meal, thank you. Here are your dishes." She indicated the bag at her feet. "I have a little info to share." Her narrative included Dr. Hays and the visits to different labs.

"I don't have much to report, but I am following a lead. My friend Evan agreed to stay at your Bainbridge house so I didn't hire any guards."

He avoided direct eye-contact and his tone seemed cold, but Anna had no emotional strength to question why.

"Did you tell FARA who you really are?"

"No." She slung her purse strap over her shoulder and stood. "I appreciate the meals you've provided, but you don't have to continue. From now on we can call or text if we have information to share."

She wasn't sure how she expected Cullen to respond, but when he also stood and nodded, her stomach muscles tightened and quashed the excited butterflies.

While driving home, Anna shelved all thoughts of Cullen. He'd helped her immensely, but her heart couldn't handle the hot and cold vibes he sent out. She rolled her eyes. Maybe he reacted to her indecisiveness.

Before preparing for bed, she checked her email. An urgent message from Dr. Faulkner sent thirty minutes ago requested she call him immediately. She sat at her desk, removed the phone from the charger and dialed his number. Deliberately crossing her ankles stopped her leg from bouncing. She needed no hyperactivity to aggravate the roiling in her stomach. Dr. Faulkner had been a marvelous mentor, but they weren't exactly friends. His call must relate to her job at FARA.

Chapter 19

"Good evening, sir. What's so urgent?"

"I assume you were accepted into FARA's training program. Since providing them an excellent reference for you, I've had second thoughts."

"About me?" Anna's mouth gaped and her shoulders sagged.

"No, no. About FARA. I have a colleague who used to work there. She, um, she's an alcoholic. To maintain her privacy, I'll call her Jill. Last evening, she shared details about her work and why she left. At the time, I figured she exaggerated her role, either to impress me or because she was slightly inebriated. But I've since given her comments a lot more thought." He paused.

Anna tapped the speaker icon on her phone so she could take notes. "What did she say, sir?"

"First, I have a question. Did you apply to work at FARA because of their genetic research?"

Without knowing what Faulkner might share, Anna wasn't about to reveal her true motives. She took a deep, calming breath. "Yes. My foray into the art world suited me for a time, but now I want to participate in the life-changing world of genetics." *That lie came too easily.*

"Have you heard of CRISPR? All caps, C, R, I, S, P, R?"

"No."

"The initials stand for Clustered Regularly Interspaced Short Palindromic Repeats."

"Still don't know."

"I won't bore you with all the details. Check the websites I'll forward to you. This information will relate back to Jill. Here are the basics. CRISPR combined with the protein complex Cas9 can act like a pair of scissors which select a part of the genome to cut, thereby removing genes within an organism."

"Whoa. Organisms…including humans?" Anna's thoughts collided with each other. Would any of Falkner's information answer Anna's driving questions?

"Yes. The procedure is controversial, but it could be used in treatments for a variety of genetic related conditions, such as cystic fibrosis."

"That's fantastic." She frowned and sobered. Faulkner didn't just want to share the benefits of this new technology. "What did Jill experience at FARA?"

"I'll get to her."

Anna jotted down his salient points. Genome editing techniques used for decades. Gene therapy procedures that deposit new genetic material but don't remove any can be lifesaving. CRISPR-Cas9 technology will make these therapies easier, cheaper, and faster, but they involve removing sequences in the genome. Which might prove beneficial but might also have unintended consequences.

Her mentor sure was taking his time to get to the point.

"Any procedure to alter genes in humans is highly regulated, many pose ethical questions, and some are even illegal. Jill insisted scientists at FARA frequently ignored restrictions, have done for years."

"Using what specific techniques?" Poised on the edge of her chair, Anna's grip on the pencil tightened.

"Jill said not only do they employ legitimate genome editing techniques that can make precise changes to the DNA code within a live cell, thus editing out disease causing genes, but they also conduct experiments outside the norm. Okay, I have to digress here. Do you know the difference between somatic cells and germline cells?"

"Of course. Germline cells are found in sperm, eggs, and embryos, and determine heritable characteristics. Somatic cells are non-reproductive cells."

"Succinctly stated. Editing the genome in a human will only affect that person. The changes will not be passed on to offspring."

"Hold on, sir. I'm taking notes." Adrenaline surged through Anna. She scribbled the new data while her heart thumped like a basketball dribbled against her ribcage. Why hadn't she discovered this crucial detail in her research? If her parents' genes had been modified, she would *not* inherit their changes. She almost jumped to her feet, then realized Faulkner asked if she was ready for him to continue.

"Please do."

"When a genome is edited in germline cells, those changes will affect said embryo and be inherited by all future generations. This procedure is highly controversial. Sure, it can eliminate disease causing genes, but the potential to produce designer babies is very real although illegal."

Anna slumped in her chair. Her parents could have... She shook her head. The technology required for the procedure wasn't available twenty-seven years ago. However, Faulkner had more to disclose. Familiar roils of anxiety invaded her stomach. "What happened at FARA?"

"Jill said they've been doing germline cell editing for...years. She didn't give me a timeframe, but indicated decades before CRISPR became common knowledge. Of course, they couldn't advertise their work or expertise because they were operating outside medical guidelines and against the law." Faulkner sighed, then continued before Anna could respond. "Jill described another level of experimentation I find hard to believe. Supposedly, she heard rumors that a group of scientists who were instrumental in the early development of FARA actually discovered a way to alter genes in adults that were then passed on to their children. In other words, editing germline cells in adults." He chuckled. "I don't know whether to believe her ridiculous accusations or not."

Forcing the tremor from her voice, Anna said, "Her allegation is extreme. If scientists could have conducted such procedures in previous decades, surely someone would have divulged the secret by now" If true, her assumption she wouldn't inherit changes made to her parents' genes went up in smoke. "Did you question Jill's assertion?"

"Naturally, but by then I think her alcohol haze was wearing off and she clammed up, refusing to discuss FARA anymore. Don't let this information deter you from working there, but I want you to know the caliber of some scientists at FARA. Be careful with whom you associate. I feel it's my duty to report what I've heard. Then the authorities can investigate."

Her sojourn at the research facility might end before it began. Anna folded her arms across her abdomen, attempting to soothe the turmoil. "I'm in the middle of my orientation week. If I pass the test and am accepted, I will keep in mind what you've divulged. Or I might quit. Thank you for the information. Anything else?"

"No, but let me know what you decide." Faulkner ended the call.

Anna blew out a breath. For a minute there she thought Jill's revelation held the answer to one of her questions, but now she was back at the starting gate. Had her genes been altered? If so, when? Before conception because her parents passed on their changes, or during the embryonic stage. Or later?

After plugging in her phone, Anna underlined Faulkner's last statement which now created a new problem. Would his report to the authorities result in the closure of FARA?

Chapter 20

Try as she might, Anna couldn't ignore the websites Dr. Faulkner forwarded to her. She spent most of the night reading and absorbing the controversial information. Sleep deprived and bleary-eyed, Anna entered the van the next morning armed with insider knowledge, and eager to complete her training.

Dr. Hays's enthusiasm for his work spilled over into his instruction. Anna paid close attention to his physical movements and noticed no change. She wondered if he'd received the treatment mentioned in the conversation she'd overheard the previous day.

The trainees visited several more labs, one where artificial heart valves were being tested. Toward the end of the day, Marcus, who had asked dozens of questions, posed one more. "Dr. Hays, you talked a lot about genetically modified animals and plants and how they benefit mankind. Um," his large Adam's apple bobbed as he swallowed. "Is anyone using CRISPR technology to genetically modify human genes to benefit society?"

Dr. Hays's chest rose as he drew in a deep breath. His normally pleasant expression slipped for a second or two. He frowned so deeply, Anna feared the furrows in his forehead might become permanent. Then his jovial expression returned. "Now, young man, that is certainly not a subject FARA will ever address." His voice held a note of iciness. He turned to look at the wall clock. "It's time to go. Follow me please."

No more conversation until they were in the van.

Raul tapped Marcus's shoulder. "What made you ask such a question?"

"Just curious. Aren't you?" Marcus glanced at Natalie then Anna.

She lowered her head so he couldn't read her expression. Dr. Hays's cold tone had told her more than his words denied. Anna would definitely share this conversation and Dr. Faulkner's information with Cullen.

If the other passengers were like Anna, they were in deep thought during the quiet return trip, but their thoughts probably didn't reach the darkness hers did. She shook off the shroud of uncertainty and to take her mind off her problems, drove home while planning her evening. Heat a frozen pizza. Study for the test. Maybe call Cullen and, if time allowed, review the paper on forgiveness and grace he had prepared.

But her plans changed as she parked in her driveway. Cullen rested against his motorbike, arms folded across his expansive chest, an insulated bag at his feet. Anna sighed, nabbed her purse and climbed out of her car. "I thought we decided you weren't going to bring me meals."

"That was your decision. I have news, and I want you to eat a good meal so you can study for your test."

"Thanks. Come in." She unlocked the door and headed to her bedroom. Determined not to let Cullen's presence affect her equilibrium, she washed her face and hands, took several calming breaths, then returned to the living room, trying to keep her heartrate steady and her expression neutral.

Cullen had the meal set out, with plates, silverware, and napkins neatly arranged on bamboo placemats. He was way too familiar with her household, but his attention to detail was a welcome touch.

"I have something to share, but, if you don't mind, I'd like to eat first." Anna sat and placed the napkin across her lap.

"Suits me." He removed clingwrap from a container filled with tomato slices and lettuce, and small bowls of condiments, set a wholewheat bun on each plate, then lifted the lid from a small casserole dish.

Rich, savory aromas rose with the steam.

"My homemade veggie burgers, fresh off the grill. Hope you like them." Once seated, Cullen waited for her to serve herself before loading his burger bun, and then he said a short prayer.

They ate without talking much. After satiating her appetite, Anna leaned back and wiped her mouth. "That was the first veggie burger I've had. If they all taste that good, it won't be my last."

A blush crept up Cullen's face as he took the last bite of his burger.

Trying to avoid his dark-eyed study of her face, Anna pushed her plate aside and described her conversation with Dr. Faulkner.

"Seem as if Jill discussed detailed scenarios." Cullen leaned back. "Although inebriated, she probably included a lot of truth in her oration. In my experience, people who are under the influence don't usually fabricate events or include specifics. Will this affect your decision to stay?"

Anna held back a retort, traced the line of stitching on the placement, and said, "No. In fact, I'm more determined than ever to find out the truth." She waited a beat or two then described the exchange between Marcus and Dr. Hays and his curt response. "You should have seen the expression that flittered across the professor's face. Annoyance tinged with fear. And when he led us to the foyer, he didn't chat as he had yesterday. To me, his uncharacteristic behavior supports the veracity of Jill's revelation."

"You might be right."

"I feel pretty confident I'll pass the test tomorrow. I can't wait to see which lab I'll be assigned."

"Please be careful. Do they treat you the same as the other trainees?"

"Yes. Why? Oh, because of their inquiry into the parents."

"Yeah." He scooted back and tapped her hand. "Hear me out. I have news which might persuade you to leave FARA. I located a death certificate for Clara Louis Schneider, dated 1950, in Munich. What was your mother's middle name?"

"I don't know. There's no name listed on any documents I have." Anna hiked her shoulders. "My middle name is Louis."

"That's an interesting twist." He withdrew a folded piece of paper from his pocket and spread it on the table. "According to birth certificate data on this timeline, Clara was born in 1907. If she is the same person, then she would have died at age forty-three."

Anna picked up the timeline, glanced at the words and numerals which seemed to blur and swirl. She threw down the paper. "Names, dates, relationships. I'm as confused as ever. Who's to say any of this information is real?" She stood and was about to usher Cullen out, when he stared at her, one eyebrow raised. "There's more?" she asked.

"Yes. Clara Louis had three children. Do you want me to follow-up on their whereabouts?"

"And add more names and dates to the mess?" Anna shook her head. "Not now. Let me work at FARA first. See what I can dig up. Based on this new information, I must discover if the portrait in the foyer at the research facility is of Clara Louis Schneider and not my mother."

~

All the late-night studying paid off. After the test Friday afternoon, Anna left the facility with the other students, confident she'd passed. Exhausted and elated at the same time, however, she overcame the urge to contact Cullen and instead, attended a one act play performed at the small theater in Port Townsend.

A light drizzle fell from low-hanging gray clouds as she entered the van Saturday morning. Natalie and Raul discussed items on the test, giving Anna more reason to believe she'd passed. Many of her answers matched those of her peers. The churning in her stomach subsided and she smiled as she checked her watch. Nine on the dot and no sign of Marcus.

The driver left anyway.

Although they questioned Marcus's absence, they were all too excited and continued to rehash the test. At the facility, Judy escorted them to their lockers. They were instructed to remove their orange lab coats along with their notebooks and then followed her to the first classroom they'd used. Her bland expression gave nothing away. She pointed to the table up front. "Set your orange coats, notebooks, and pens here, please."

After complying, Anna perched on the edge of her seat, heartbeat thumping in her ears.

Arms folded, Judy eyed the students. "I see Marcus chose not to join us today. Too bad, because he scored the highest." Her lips twitched in a brief smile. "In fact, you all passed. Congratulations."

Not sure how much joy to express, Anna grinned and clasped her hands to keep from applauding.

Raul let out a loud whistle and leaned back while Natalie burst into tears.

"Let's get started. I have a lot to cover this morning." Judy seemed to ignore their reactions and opened her briefcase and removed four folders. She handed one to each trainee and set the last one on the table. "These documents detail your terms of employment and at the end is your contract which must be signed in my presence. You will receive a copy for your records at the end of the day. After I review other details, I'll give you time to read them. On Monday morning, you will make your own transportation arrangements. You can drive your personal vehicle, carpool, but no one can drop you off." Judy glanced at Anna.

When Raul and Natalie did too, Anna murmured, "Okay, no *boyfriend*."

The instruction continued. "The entrance to FARA is seven and a half miles from our former meeting place in Uncas, and four and a half from Quilcene. The officer at the security gate will let you in this once, but in future, your thumbprint will be scanned. Park in the lot directly in front of the main doors. On Monday, you will be given a parking permit which will identify your permanent spot in the parking garage." Judy paced the room. "You will be met by an employee who will take you to your assigned lab where you will be issued your coat and badge. Your photographs and thumbprint will be taken in here later this morning. Your badge is your lifeline and *will not* be removed from this facility."

Raul raised his hand and blurted out, "Will we get out tests back so we can see our scores?"

Shaking her head and frowning, Judy loomed over Raul. "Are you paying attention?

"Yes, ma'am." He blinked. "Well, will we?"

"Scores will be mailed to you, but not the actual tests." She listed more dos and don'ts and emphasized the dire consequences for breaking the rules. "All new employees are on a six-week probation. During that time your work hours will be nine to five, and then your schedule will be determined by your lab supervisor. For the most part, you will only work in one lab, but if the need arises, you will be reassigned. You may now read your paperwork. If you have any questions, direct them to me."

Anna had a dozen, but Judy's stiff body language and scowl curtailed her inquiry. She read page after page of legal jargon. Although nothing jumped out at her as being suspect, she would ask Jerome to read the contract.

A subtle knock at the door. Judy opened it and bent to listen to the suited man gesturing wildly. She closed the door and leaned against it, her face ashen.

By now, the trainees focused on Judy whose legs seemed to wobble as she approached the table. She slumped into the chair. "I just received sad news. Marcus was killed in a car accident last night."

Amidst her peers' expressions of surprise and sorrow, all Anna could think of was Marcus's question on CRISPR and Dr. Hays's reaction. Sharing her real parentage with FARA now seemed like a suicidal idea.

Chapter 21

Although Cullen had texted Anna Friday morning to say he would pray for her success on the test, she hadn't responded. Nor had she shared whether or not she'd passed, and therefore possibly a FAFA employee. Keeping in mind her request for no more meals and no more personal contact, he'd concentrated on research the past two days.

Good news and bad news. According to her birth certificate, Frida Dietrich, AKA Judy Coates, immigrated to the USA with her parents in 1977. She married Zach Coates in 2001 and they had one son. No apparent suspicious activity—she probably just changed her first name. She'd been employed at FARA for fifteen years.

Eager for his next research targets to produce more interesting discoveries, he'd used the names of the seven people listed on the piece of paper from Claire's condo which William verified were scientists who recently died. Alas, he found no connection with the Das Institut. Naturally, they could have changed their names as Claire and Hugh had, but since all the documents were in German and translator apps were time consuming, he concluded that line was a dead-end.

To cheer himself and eat a good meal, he'd played his guitar for diners at Tom's restaurant for several hours.

Saturday's research revealed more constructive details. At least, he hoped Anna would agree with his assessment. Using data from the timeline, and after hours of deep dives into specialized search engines, he located records for Clara and Hugo and their three children, possibly Anna's siblings. Although Anna had shown no interest in discovering a connection, he continued. Maybe these relatives could answer Anna's burning questions.

The children were born after Clara signed on to work at Das Institut. A son, Karl, in 1935, and fraternal twins, Therese and Paul, in 1937. If still living, they'd be in their 80s, with grandchildren, even great-grandchildren. Surely, Anna would want that information. However, further investigation revealed Karl died in1944, and Paul in 1957. Next, he concentrated on Therese Ritter. No death certificate for her under that name. Cullen's usual searches located no marriage certificate, nor records of any children.

Late in the afternoon, he discovered she immigrated to the USA and married Cecil Edwards in 1969. All interesting details. He closed his laptop, then carried his Bible and a glass of iced water outside to the patio. He had a message to prepare for Sunday's service in Port Hadlock.

Although the passage he chose in Romans 12:9–10 needed little elaboration, he couldn't focus. Anna and FARA and his recent research occupied too much of his mind. He leaned back and closed his eyes.

A tap on his shoulder and soft words woke him.

"Cullen, I have to talk to you, please."

He straightened and gazed up at Anna. He couldn't help but grin. Just the person he wanted to see. "Have a seat. Can I get you anything to drink?"

Anna scooted a chair closer to him. "No, thanks."

At first, he thought her woeful expression indicated she failed the test, but when tears pooled in her eyes, he figured she had more on her mind. "What's wrong?"

"I've been home a while, but I can't handle this by myself."

"What happened?"

She sucked in a breath. "Marcus was killed last night. Car wreck." She swiped at her cheeks. "But I don't believe it was an accident."

"Tell me." Cullen took her hand.

"Obviously, I have no proof, just gut instinct."

"You think he got too close to the truth by asking about modifications to human genes?"

Anna nodded, her gray eyes glistening. He noticed the flecks around her pupils darkened to match her mood. She pulled her hand free and stood. "I talked with Lexie briefly, but they're short-staffed so she's busy at their restaurant. You're the only person who understands what this could mean."

The tremor in her voice galvanized him. He rose and drew her into a hug. She melted against his chest, and he sighed. The desire to keep her safe, not only now, but long-term, filled his heart. He'd never felt the strong need to protect someone since his disastrous relationship with Krissy Laing. How could Anna have dented his armor in such a short time? On the verge of declaring his feelings, he released her as she pushed him away, almost as if she read his mind.

She folded her arms and took a couple of steps

backward. "I passed the test."

"Great. I knew you would." Cullen returned to his chair in an effort to disguise his emotions. He wanted to hold her, kiss away her hurt. "But you don't sound too happy."

"I'm fighting the desire to work at FARA with the knowledge they can be ruthless and unethical."

He sensed she needed him to be a sounding board. "I know you still want to find out about your genes and prospects for a longer than usual lifespan. Especially after hearing from Faulkner."

"Yes. I *must* find out. Don't try to convince me to leave."

An admonition almost spilled from his mouth, but he changed direction at the last moment. "That could take a long time. What about your commitment to the art institute?"

Anna sat on the edge of her chair. "Come fall semester, I'll have to return. That gives me two months. If investigating on my own fails, I will consider telling them who my parents were."

Straining at the self-imposed reins on his tongue, Cullen said in a tone he hoped was non-judgmental, "Sounds as if you've decided on your path forward. I suppose it would be useless for me to dissuade you from divulging your parentage." He held up a hand when she attempted to speak. "Please, Anna, if you do decide to tell FARA, let me know. A text will do."

She looked beyond him for a few seconds, then smiled briefly. "Agreed. Although we didn't discover why Mother left half her fortune to the Nachwelt Foundation, I think I can handle my future on my own. I showed my FARA contract to Jerome Jennings this morning. He found nothing suspect. I asked him to end your contract. I don't think there's anything else you can do for me."

The words struck Cullen like a dagger to the gut. If Anna no longer needed his computer skills, how could he protect her? Although he didn't require a contract to do that, but it would help if he had a legitimate reason to be in her company. To seek her out.

Aha. He had the perfect news to change her mind. "I conducted a lot of research recently. Can I share my findings?"

"Sure. Then I need to leave."

He told her about Judy's background and the FARA employees who'd died and had no connection to Das Institut. "However, I have other information that might help in your gene modification quest. I discovered Clara and Hugh had three children during the early years of their marriage in Germany."

First, she frowned, then she leaned back. "Carry on."

He shared the details concerning their births and the deaths of the two boys. "Therese immigrated to the USA in 1969."

Anna stared at him, mouth agape.

"But I found a death certificate for Therese Edwards, nee Ritter, dated 1983."

"She died at age, what, forty-six?"

No reprimand for doing research she'd asked him not to. "Right. I can find out if she had any kids. Much easier searching records in English." He smiled, but she didn't react. Not sure what rambled through her mind, he drained his glass.

She sat in silence for ten, fifteen seconds. Without

looking at him, she asked, "How will that help me exactly? If this Therese person was still alive, I could ask about her...our parents. Show her pictures of Claire and Hugh to see if they were indeed Clara and Hugo. What am I supposed to do with this information?"

"I can continue researching. Maybe locate her husband, children. Family photo albums." Although Anna's face reddened to the point he thought he might have to douse her in cold water, he couldn't help himself. He waffled on. "I had to stop my online work to prepare for my lesson for tomorrow. By the way, I'll be meeting with a small group in Port Hadlock. Would you like to join me? I know Lexie has been studying the Bible with you and she told me your mother was an atheist. I'm sure you have lots of questions, and I want to help you." He immediately regretted mentioning her mother and rubbed his chin.

Turning to him, Anna said through gritted teeth, "I specifically asked you not to conduct any research on possible siblings. You want to control my life. What I eat, where I work, and now you want to take control over my spiritual life, too. I'm on a precipice and I need guidance, but not what you offer." She stood, eyes narrowed. "I'll make sure Jerome has funds to pay you, and then I never want to see you again." Purse strap slung over her shoulder, she stormed to her car. Gravel churned up from the tires as she reversed.

He knew his eyebrows rose and his eyes bugged. Controlling? His sisters often accused him of trying to be the General Manager of the Universe. Maybe they weren't joking. His take-charge attitude could be why he'd never had a serious relationship for many years. One outburst from Anna, and his past associations with women paraded before his eyes. But what was wrong with wanting to keep people safe? That's all he desired for Anna. She was about to walk into a den of vipers and every gigabyte of knowledge he had couldn't protect her when he had no access to the facility.

Turing to the book of Romans, Cullen sighed. He did want to address her spiritual needs, but he had no idea his presence overwhelmed her.

Chapter 22

Monday morning dawned gray and drizzly, but no inclement weather dampened Anna's excitement. Even reviewing her disastrous meeting with Cullen Saturday afternoon and her indecisive actions Sunday did nothing to suppress her anticipation. She'd wanted to attend Cullen's church service in Port Hadlock and apologize, but she also wanted to maintain the belief she no longer needed his services. The latter option won. In between grocery shopping and house cleaning yesterday, she'd indulged in a long hike, and never once opened her laptop.

Anna parked in the designated area outside the FARA facility and dashed inside. Ten minutes early. She wondered if Dr. Faulkner had reported the facility, but all seemed normal. He'd not responded to her email stating she'd passed the test and asking if he'd followed through with his threat. The receptionist handed her a badge and made a phone call. A few minutes later, a short, squat woman wearing a lime green lab coat opened one of the security doors and beckoned Anna.

"Good morning, Miss Knight. I'm Georgina Jones, your supervisor for the duration of your probationary period."

They entered an elevator Anna hadn't used before and exited on sub-level two.

"You will be working in one of our cancer research labs. Come this way."

Anna followed the middle-aged woman who swiped her badge and opened the lab door.

"Wear your coat along with your badge at all times. Before you go home, check them in at the front desk. Do not attempt to remove either from the facility." All said in a bland tone as if Georgina had made the spiel many times. She handed Anna a maroon coat and a thin binder. "Your job description, lists of expectations. I'll be available most of the time if you have any questions."

Thankful for Judy's in-depth training, Anna successfully completed her first day. Initially disappointed with her assignment, she soon accepted her lot and threw herself into the job. Although week one ended without her garnering any new information, she did see more of the facility. Her days were filled preparing supplies for experiments, charting results, and data entry, or delivering sealed reports to other labs. However, her movements were restricted to sub-levels one and two, but maybe she'd be more successful in the coming weeks of her probationary period.

In lieu of sharing her experiences with Cullen, she documented each day's activities in a journal. People she met, co-workers, noting anything she thought might help her to explore the facility at a later time. She indicated her surprise at not seeing Raul or Natalie and regretted she hadn't obtained their contact information during training. Maybe Cullen could...

Late one night as Anna straightened items on her

desk, the handout he'd prepared poked out from under a stack of books. She stared at it and shook her head. How did it get there? Last time she handled the paper she'd placed it in a drawer. Blame it on brain fog or excitement about her job. But since the page seemed to call out her name, she sat at the desk and reviewed the points Cullen made on forgiveness and grace. Although tempted to attend the midweek Bible study, Anna reneged. She was not ready to face Cullen and beg *his* forgiveness, let alone delving into how she could accept God's grace.

Taking advantage of a stress-free weekend, Anna completed her abstract ocean scene painting, and although not totally satisfied, set it aside, but determined to try the style again. While dusting the living room furniture, she knelt beside the coffee table and fingered Papa's chess pieces. She'd often watched him and a friend play and wanted desperately to be included. Papa's reply was always the same, "When you are older, my Annika, I'll teach you the game."

That day never came. She gently placed the marble pieces in the designated slots on the sides of the board and wondered if Cullen played. Maybe he could teach her. Nope. But the thought of him brought back memories of their eventful association. Family research, documents located, and so much more.

Reminded of other items she rescued from the Bainbridge house, Anna dashed to the laundry room and retrieved the jewelry box she'd hidden there two weeks ago. She tossed aside the dish towel and, for the first time, examined the intricately carved wood. About the size of a cigar box, garlands of leaves decorated the sides, and roses covered the top of the heavy piece. The lid lifted easily to expose a green velvet lined interior. No jewels. Only an envelope.

Anna sat at the dining table, removed the envelope from the box and opened it. She unfolded the single sheet of cream-colored stationary which looked to be in pristine condition, as if no one had ever read it. The precise handwritten German script contained several tiny black ink blots. Anna scanned the letter dated October, 1939, signed by Clara, with a postscript. The page fluttered to the table.

Hands over her chest to soothe her thumping heart, Anna stared at the missive. A note from Clara. She translated as she read. "This box is too...precious for me to display now. It was given to me by my...grandmother for my tenth birthday. She had it specially made, a...an accomplishment considering the Great War was in progress. The...artist, no, artisan, Rolf Hoffman, appreciated the business."

Anna turned over the box and found the initials *RH* etched into the base. Heart still on a wild gallop, she studied the undated postscript. The handwriting varied a little from the body of the letter, and it appeared to have been written with a ballpoint pen. "One day, I will give the box to Annika."

No amount of outside pressure could rein in the frantic beats of her heart. She rose, paced to the kitchen and back, then drew in a calming breath and returned to her chair. Did two people write the letter, Clara the first part and Claire the postscript? Or, was the whole letter written by the same person, the difference in handwriting due to her age?

Faced with the question that had gnawed at her insides for weeks, Anna picked up her phone to call

Cullen, but recalled her resolution in time. She placed the jewelry box with the chess set, slipped Clara's letter into her journal, and continued her chores. She would find answers on her own.

~

During the second week at FARA, Anna met Danny Young. He also wore a maroon coat and had worked in the lab next door where they concentrated on cancers that affected children. His badge indicated he had access to sub-level three. They often worked on the same projects and frequently ate lunch together. When questioned about labs on the lower level, he pursed his lips and shook his head.

"Sorry. Just curious. I don't want to alienate you." Anna swirled another shrimp in cocktail sauce.

"No problem. But you know what they say. If I told you, I'd have to kill you." Danny's grin softened his words.

So far, Anna had been unable to garner any details about the facility or the work done from her colleagues. Maybe Danny's threat held more truth than mirth.

On Wednesday while in the cafeteria, he asked her on a date. Although fun to work with, she declined, stating a recent break up as her reason, which wasn't a complete lie. Anna had yet to bring her own lunch. Instead, she enjoyed the variety available, meals she had no idea how to prepare. She did miss Cullen's contribution to her healthy diet. Oh, well. It had been her choice to end the relationship. But they could be friends.

Once the idea solidified, Anna decided to attend the Bible study at Tom and Lexie's restaurant. She would apologize to Cullen and maybe he'd answer the questions she had on grace. Showered, sundress donned, and contacts in, she drove to the restaurant. She scanned the circle of participants. No Cullen. When Lexie sat beside her, she asked, "Is Cullen coming?"

Lexie shrugged. "I don't know. He didn't call me or Tom." She turned toward Anna and her eyebrows rose. "Do I detect disappointment? Ladybug, are you forming a romantic interest in him?"

"No. Of course not." Heat rose up her neck and into her cheeks.

"Ooh, protesting and blushing. He's a great catch and you two would make a perfect pair."

"Stop, Lexie. I'm...too busy for romance."

"Hmm. If you say so. Anyway, I have to tell you what happened last week."

Leaning close, Anna stared at her friend.

"Before Tom led the study, Cullen asked for the floor. He apologized for trying to be in control of every situation and for interfering in people's lives by imposing his ideas and ignoring their wishes." She took Anna's hand. "I tell you, I've never seen the man so contrite, so humble."

Tom joined the group and sat on the other side of Lexie. "Let's begin. We have a special guest this evening. My college friend, Brian Mosely, will lead our singing."

As sweet words of praise surrounded Anna, she closed her eyes. Surely other people in Cullen's life through the years had objected to his actual or attempted level of control. Did he pay heed to her criticism? If so, why?

Tom continued his lesson on the Armor of God, which he'd begun the previous week. Anna located the reference from Ephesians 6:11 on her cell phone app and followed along, but determined to purchase a printed Bible with a concordance, similar to what Lexie used. Her friend's studies with her had laid the foundation upon which Anna now wanted to build in her search for forgiveness, grace, and salvation. The time spent with the group of believers, especially Lexie and Tom, refreshed Anna's soul.

Dismissed from FARA late Friday afternoon, Anna hurried to the front desk to deliver her coat and badge. The security guard held an animated conversation on the phone, and mouthed toward her, "I'll be with you in a minute."

She set her items on the counter and turned to view the huge portraits. A woman wearing a navy-blue lab coat, which Anna knew by now indicated an upper echelon employee, stood in front of Clara's picture and stared at it as if studying the masterpiece for flaws. From the back, her blonde chignon resembled Mother's. No big deal, but when she muttered, "What were you thinking, Clara?" Anna covered her gasp with a cough and approached the woman who shoved her hands into her pockets and headed toward the other security door. Curiosity overcame protocol and Anna followed.

"Hey, you can't go in there." The guard hurried around the counter, and, if his tone and demeanor were anything to go by, ready to tackle Anna to the ground.

"Sorry." She halted. "I think I know that person. I was—"

"That's a restricted entry point. I have to report this incident." He ushered Anna back to the counter and kept his eyes on her as he returned to his post.

"Look. I didn't break any rules. I was going to call out to her before she ever reached the door." Anna had to persuade the guard to change his mind. A demerit at this point might get her fired.

The guard huffed out a breath. "All right, Ms. Knight. I concede I was distracted by the phone call. I won't make an official report this time."

Anna squelched her sigh of relief. No point letting him know how scared she'd been. She changed tactics. "Do you know that woman? Can you tell me her name?"

"I do, but I can't. Security, et cetera. You understand, right?"

"Yes. Thanks. See you next week." Anna strode out of the building and entered the parking garage. Obviously, the scientist knew something important about Clara. Come next week, Anna would be more aggressive in asking questions.

After completing Saturday chores, Anna attempted another abstract painting. The Hugh Knight Institute of Art hosted an exhibition of staff and students' works the second weekend of July. So far, Anna only had one piece to show. But try as she might, her brushes wouldn't cooperate.

She removed her smock and threw it across the room. "You've only got one week, Annika Louis. You'd better get your imagination in gear."

Harrumphing, she sat at her desk and opened her laptop. After ordering a Bible, she responded to email messages. Dr. Faulkner still hadn't acknowledged her email. Maybe he changed his mind, or the authorities didn't believe the accusations.

She collected her mail from the box at the end of

her short drive. Several pieces of junk mail and Papa's death certificate. She returned to her desk and opened the large envelope.

Cause of death—catastrophic organ failure. Date of birth—April 10, 1951. Parents—Nigel and Alice Knight. Other than the cause of his death and the date, Anna didn't believe the rest of the information. Born in 1951, died in 2001, at age fifty. Sure. She glanced at Papa's photo on the mantel. He looked much older. And, she made a mental bet, if Cullen researched Nigel and Alice Knight, he probably wouldn't find a record of them anywhere. Thinking of Cullen, she wished she'd kept the timeline he'd made of her family.

Instead of allowing her suspicions about Hugo and Clara to overwhelm her again, Anna retreated to the sofa, closed her eyes, and recalled one of her last memories of Papa. Sitting on his lap and finding the crucifix he wore. Had he also been an atheist and later experienced a change of heart? Did he apologize for saddling her with gene manipulation?

Maybe she would never find the answers she sought about her physical body, but, taking a leaf out of Papa's book, she could seek solutions to her spiritual dilemmas. She had previously made a cursory study of the handout Cullen had provided on forgiveness and God's grace, but this time she spent a couple of hours reading the Scriptures he listed and weighed them against her feelings of inadequacy. In spite of recognizing her failures, she drew closer to accepting God's grace.

Relaxing on the sofa, she closed the Bible app on her phone. She needed to act on what she'd read and now believed. Her thoughts immediately flew to

Cullen. And his Sunday practice of leading worship in little communities around Port Townsend. She didn't want to call and ask him where he'd be tomorrow in case she changed her mind. Instead, she showered, slipped on jeans and a T-shirt, then drove to Tom's restaurant. Although she had a refrigerator full of food, she had no desire to cook.

Lexie was overjoyed to see her. "Come here, ladybug. Give me a hug."

Enveloped in her friend's arms, vestiges of anxiety from her afternoon discovery melted away. "I can see you're busy."

"Not like previous weeks. Tom hired two waitstaff and a line cook."

"Great. Can you sit with me while I eat?"

"Sure. I'll submit your order then join you for a little while."

Anna sat in the courtyard at a table for two and sipped her iced water.

A few minutes later, Lexie plopped down in the other chair and set her elbows on the table. "You look different this evening. What's happened? Are you still at the, um, new job?"

"Yes. No major discoveries yet, but I have something else to discuss. I...I've been so focused on my parents and what I might have physically inherited from them that I have neglected Biblical truths you shared with me years ago. I know you pray for my soul, and I appreciate that you've never forced any of your beliefs on me." Anna blew out a breath. "This is harder than I anticipated. Anyway, I want to visit whatever group Cullen will worship with tomorrow so I can ask him questions about God's grace. Do you know where he'll be?"

Lexie clasped both Anna's hands and squeezed. "Oh, my precious ladybug. I rejoice along with the angels. Cullen stopped by last evening. He had a new client and that's why he didn't come for the Bible study. He'll be in Chimacum tomorrow, about twenty miles south. I have the address in the office. I'll text you." She released Anna's hands and stood. "I am beyond happy for you, friend. And I'll keep you in my prayers." Walking backward to the doors, Lexie waved then placed her hands together in the praying gesture.

Returning the wave, Anna smiled and waited for her meal.

Appetite satiated and the Chimacum address on her phone, Anna strolled to the outdoor concert venue along the waterfront. Unfortunately, she arrived as the lead singer gestured the crowd to hush, and he said, "Thank you for being a great audience. I'll repeat our philosophy I stated when we began. My brothers and I are not ashamed to admit we are patriots and Christians. Our last number is always our signature rendition of "God Bless America". Stand and sing along if you so desire, or just sit and absorb the beautiful words."

Although Anna didn't join in, she allowed the words of the song to sink into her mind and soul. In this troubled world, the country needed God. So did she.

Chapter 23

Alerted by Lexie that Anna might attend the service this morning, Cullen looked up every time someone entered the living room. Evan and his wife had asked him to speak at their home church and had arranged chairs around the large living room.

Cullen sat facing the door and played a medley of worship tunes. Three empty chairs remained. Five minutes before ten, Anna entered. He immediately set down his guitar and approached her. Adrenaline buzzed through his body and his heartbeat accelerated. He didn't care that his grin spread from ear to ear. Leaning close, he whispered, "Glad to see you. Can we talk after the service?"

When she sat and nodded, he mentally pumped the air with a fist, and returned to his seat. All the while Evan led the service, Cullen's eyes never strayed far from Anna. There was something different about her. Not physically, but more her demeanor. She appeared calm, settled.

Evan had asked Cullen to address the topic of grace. He began with the lesson he'd given at the weekly Bible study group then added words from Titus 2:11. "The Apostle Paul teaches us God's grace is available to all. After we accept grace, we need to live a self-controlled, upright, and godly life. However, we are human, and we will fall. Slip. Dare I say, sin. Then what happens to us? Will we be outside grace? Some people believe this concept and live a yoyo existence. In. Out. In. Out. They live in constant fear they might die when they are *outside* grace."

He rubbed his temples with both hands. "That's enough to give anyone a headache. And a heart ache." Holding up his Bible, he said, "But that is not how God wants us to live. That's not what He promised. To conclude, I'll use an analogy and apologize in advance to those who are not football fans. Consider the King Dome that used to house our Seattle Seahawks. You are a participant in the game. Your job is to play to the best of your ability. Stay inbounds. Follow the rules. You have coaches on the sidelines instructing you. Fans in the bleachers encouraging you. Or enemies trying to get you to play a different game."

Many attendees nodded.

"You get my point. As a player, life happens, and you drift out of bounds. You…sin. Oh, no. You are benched. You are lost. Can you get back into grace?" He eyed the audience. "Yes. Because of your obedience to Christ, you are always in grace. Back to the football field. Many people believe that grace only exists *on* the playing field, within the painted lines. But grace is the whole stadium of your life. Sure, you need to get back onto the field and follow the teachings of Christ. That's what being a Christian means. The Bible is our playbook, so to speak."

A chorus of "amens" rippled through the group.

"Live in the state of grace. It's your home. Don't

just visit the state as if on vacation." Cullen pointed to his Bible. "I'll close with a reminder from Romans 3:23–24. I'll paraphrase. We all have sinned, but we are all justified—made right, vindicated, validated—by God's grace."

Picking up his guitar, he added, "I pray you have been blessed by the word of God." He strummed a few chords as Evan led the closing prayer.

People milled about the room, some shook Cullen's hand and thanked him for his insight, but the person he wanted to see had disappeared. He made his way outside and found Anna leaning against her car. "There you are. I thought you'd gone."

"No. I need to talk to you."

"Great. Would you like to join me for lunch?" He wanted to take her arm and lead her to his motorbike, but held back remembering his vow to be less controlling. Especially with her. He waited.

A shadow flitted across her face, but she said, "Okay. Where?"

"I know a place—" *Let go of the reins.* "You tell me. Your choice."

"A new little restaurant opened last week in Port Townsend. It's on Hudson Street."

"Text me the address, and after I collect my belongings and say farewell to Evan, I'll meet you in town. By the way, he's the guy who coordinated the repairs to the office in your mother's house. Do you want to chat with him? He'd like—"

"Maybe another day."

"Okay." Not sure why, but he reached for her hand and shook it.

Another unusual expression crossed her face. He

pivoted and strode into the house.

Guitar case strapped to the back of his bike, Cullen rode to the restaurant. During the past two weeks, he'd resisted the desire to call Anna, or to stop by her house after her shift at FARA. He parked his bike, removed his helmet, and studied the gravel at his feet. He'd missed her. Not Anna the client, but Anna the woman. Finally admitting this truth released the boa constrictor that seemed to have installed itself around his life.

Drawing in a deep breath, he entered the café. *Don't blow it, Kincaid.*

The mealtime conversation touched on mundane topics, but Cullen couldn't keep his curiosity in check. He asked, "What do you want to discuss?"

She moved aside her half-eaten clam linguini and placed her forearms on the table. "Not here. Can we walk along the beach when you're done?"

"I'm ready now." He beckoned for the waiter to bring the bill. "Since we might be gone a while, can I leave my guitar in your car?"

"Sure. I'll open the trunk for you."

The trek to the beach took all of five minutes. Cullen almost bit a chunk out of his tongue waiting for her to speak first.

She pointed to a large piece of driftwood and sat. One knee bounced rapidly a few seconds then she straightened her legs and crossed her ankles.

Cullen sat beside her, hands clasped to keep them from reaching out to her.

Finally, she huffed out a breath and gazed at the gentle waves lapping the shore. "I have a lot to say. First, I haven't gathered any new information from FARA. Their security is Fort Knox-tight, but one of my colleagues, Danny Young, might be a good resource in time. I'm keeping a journal of my day-to-day activities."

"That's a great idea."

After throwing him a quick glance, she continued. "I found a letter in the jewelry box written by Clara in 1939." She drew an envelope from her purse and handed it to him. "See for yourself. She says the box was a special gift, but the part that affects me is the postscript."

Cullen unfolded the letter and studied the German words. A name popped out to him. "She mentions you."

"Yes. She was going to give me the letter. The handwriting is not quite the same. What do you think?"

"Clara wrote the body of the letter in 1939, and Claire added the postscript after you were born." He faced Anna. "Or, the same person wrote it all."

Standing, Anna set her hands on her hips. "Exactly what I surmised. Proof, at least in my estimation, my parents did indeed undergo gene modification." She turned toward him and ran her fingers through her hair from the mid-part down the left side of her face. "See this strand of white?"

"Yeah. I really didn't think much about it as many people have colorful streaks in their hair these days. However, sometimes yours is not as pronounced as it is today."

"Right. I added a bit of color when I interviewed for the job and consequently every time I go to FARA. People who knew my mother might make a connection since she had a similar streak."

"Quick thinking."

"I can be innovative. Anyway, it's a genetic

anomaly. This part of my hair lacks melanin, therefore, has no color. And guess what? Whoever painted the large portrait of Clara included her white streak. I wonder if she was lefthanded too. I also inherited that trait from Mother." Anna shrugged and smiled.

Not the reaction he expected. He rose and handed her the letter. "You seem to have accepted that reality." Her calm attitude and even tone were all devoid of anger, panic, and uncertainty.

"I have. Now I must find out what I can concerning my future. I have four weeks left in my probationary employment. My fulltime assignment might provide more opportunities. However, as I stated previously, if by mid-August, I haven't found answers to my questions, I will tell FARA who my parents were. If the scientists there can't provide what I need, then no one can."

Although Cullen wanted to take her in his arms and insist she quit her job, he settled for touching her shoulder. "Let's walk."

She grabbed her purse and strode beside him.

"You know I would prefer you leave FARA now, but—" He held out a hand to ward off her objection. "I understand your need and I only have one request." Choosing his words with care, he shoved his hands in his pockets. "I know I've asked before, but please keep me updated. We don't have to meet but you can call, text anytime."

"I will."

"Be careful. Remember, I just want you to be safe." He swallowed many other admonitions and he hoped she noticed his attempts to be less controlling, but he couldn't help himself. "Could you check in each evening? A quick text, especially after you tell them about your parents."

"Okay." She rolled her eyes.

"One more thing. This might sound paranoid, but can we choose a code word you'll use if you feel threatened? A word or phrase easy to include in a conversation."

"Really, Cullen, is that necessary?"

"Indulge me, please."

Frowning, she said, "How about 'new lab coat'? I could legitimately use that phrase."

"Perfect."

"Thanks for caring." Her steps slowed. "One more item about my parentage. May I have the timeline you made?"

"Certainly. I'll drop it off this afternoon."

"Great. I received Papa's death certificate and need to add his details."

"Anything unusual about it?"

"I'll show you when you come by." Anna walked closer to the water. "Come, Mr. Kincaid. I have something else to discuss."

Two of his steps and he'd caught up with her. Driftwood decorated the stony beach. To keep from tossing a dozen questions at Anna, Cullen counted the logs. Six...seven...eight...

"I have a lot more on my mind." She stepped over a large chunk of wood. "I'm sure you are aware that Lexie studied the Bible with me while at university and since graduation. More recently, I've reviewed in great detail the handout you provided on forgiveness and grace. You know my mother was an atheist, so I began this journey with a skewed view of God. Which brings me to another very personal revelation."

Her pause lasted only a few seconds, but Cullen thought the sun would set before she continued.

"For as long as I can remember, Mother and I had a strained relationship. My interest in drawing and painting met with her disdain, which led me to join a graffiti group in Seattle. Landed me ninety days in Juvie."

"I didn't—"

"I squelched my artistic desires and tried to accept her path for me. But she never believed I was smart enough to follow in her footsteps. In an attempt to gain her approval with good grades, I resorted to using amphetamines in college. Of course, that didn't work. The drugs increased my panic attacks, and it wasn't until a caring instructor convinced me to seek professional help that I was diagnosed with an anxiety disorder."

Cullen had to comment. "I know a little about the subject through a cousin. You are doing a great job handling your symptoms. I, um, can see how my attempts to help, or control you and your situations didn't sit well."

"Right. Although I appreciate the research data you've collected and your concern for my well-being, I'm easily overwhelmed when people try to make decisions for me without including my input. That action can trigger my anxiety, and I've worked too hard to return to my miserable college days."

"I had no idea." He shook his head. If he'd known sooner, he would have acted differently. "How do you cope, day-to-day?"

"Prescribed medication and following a four-step

process which I call CALM. C: count slowly while inhaling, exhaling. A: analyze the situation. What brought on the episode? I prefer not to use the words 'panic attack'. L: look for something positive to focus on. Flowers, the stars, a dog, a baby. You'll be surprised what you can see when you're searching. M: move. Take a walk, go for a jog, ride a bike. At first, I had to go through all four steps, but now when I recognize the onset of an episode, I can combine the steps quickly, almost as one. Controlled breathing, analysis, positive aspects, and movement."

They reached the end of the walkable section of beach. Cullen said, "Let's turn around."

"Okay." She was on a roll and picked up the thread of her conversation. "You can imagine Mother was not supportive at all. She blamed my condition on my lack of mental strength. Only weak people succumbed to mental disorders. As if the diagnosis reflected on her. By—"

"Whoa, whoa." Cullen halted and Anna stopped beside him. "I'm surprised you haven't made the connection. As the product of two humans who'd undergone gene modification, maybe your mother expected you to be perfect." She squinted at him. "Um, her expectations, not mine."

Anna gazed at her feet, then out to sea, and finally back to him. "You're making my brain hurt. We can continue that discussion another time. I want to, no, need to complete what I have to say. Please."

Nodding, Cullen began walking again.

"By the time I entered graduate school and met Lexie, Mother knew I was studying the Bible. She threw the usual comments my way. If there was a God, why did He let me suffer? I had no answers, but her remarks added to my feelings of unworthiness. Which in turn led me to question God forgiving me of my past. Fast forward to this morning." She slipped her arm through his and he bent his elbow.

Although a cool wind blew briny air off the ocean, his blood heated to near boiling, sending his heart into a tailspin.

"Last night I wrote down questions I had on grace and how we can be sure we are covered."

Cullen physically slapped his hand over his mouth. Not wanting to interfere with her train of thought, he only muttered, "Uh-huh."

"Then you used that example of our lives being a stadium and grace covers the whole thing." She gave his arm a squeeze. "Thank you."

"That analogy came to me last night. Did it help?"

"Definitely. At least as far as grace is concerned. But I have a few questions about forgiveness, which are probably connected to grace. Here goes. Soon after we met, you mentioned you have a hard time accepting God's forgiveness. If you feel that way, then how can I expect to understand? Do we have to forgive ourselves before God forgives us? How does that work?"

"You sure are delving deep into these subjects, young lady. I'll share what I came to realize while studying for the mid-week Bible study. Self-forgiveness is an important part in the healing process. It allows us to let go of any anger, guilt, or shame associated with our past actions. We must accept that we will make mistakes. Remember the scripture I read from Romans 3:23? We've all sinned and fallen short. We are not perfect, that is why Christ died for us. To make us perfect in the sight of God by washing away our sins. While on this earth, we are a work in progress, but we must try to live a sin-free life." He set his hand over his heart, sure the beating was from the wings of the Holy Spirit in the form a dove. "The hymn 'Amazing Grace' reminds us no one is so far from God that His grace can't reach us."

Strolling arm-in-arm, they returned to the spot where they began. He wasn't sure Anna had said everything she'd planned, and he wouldn't force any decisions from her, but he had to ask, "Do you have any other questions?

She nodded. "I understand what we've discussed, but how do I reconcile working at FARA under false pretenses with trying to follow Christ?"

"I admire you for the amount of thought you've devoted to this subject." He patted her hand resting on his forearm. "Here is the advice I give myself and what I've offered to other folks. We can't change what we did or said in the past, but we should make amends if we can. Our goal must be to follow Jesus's teachings from this day forward, to the best of our abilities. Repent when we sin and know God's grace covers us."

Her shoulders sagged. "Oh, what a mess. I provided false information about my parents, and I don't intend to work there very long."

"One last bit of advice to dwell on, provided by Jesus himself. In the eighth chapter of John's Gospel, we read about the woman caught in adultery. The pharisees were ready to stone her to death. Jesus told the group that if anyone was without sin, he could cast the first stone. One by one the accusers left. Then Jesus told the woman to go and leave her life of sin. Another version says, "Go and sin no more." I like that."

"Me too." She blew out a deep breath. "Thank you."

They crossed the street and Cullen couldn't leave the discussion without asking, "Are you ready to make a commitment?"

"Not at the moment. It's getting late and I need to work on another entry for the art exhibition."

He'd studied the path of salvation with enough people to know the next step had to come from her. Although he'd like nothing more than to spend the rest of the afternoon with her to continue their Bible study, he accepted her excuse or reason. But he had to build on their reestablished association which she had instigated. "Will you attend the July 4th celebration tomorrow evening?"

"Maybe after work."

"I'll be here. The fireworks will be displayed from two barges out in the bay and a large section of Water Street will be blocked to traffic."

"I remember the crowds last year."

She made no attempt to arrange a meeting so he nixed his question. Sharing her soul with him had been awesome, but she hadn't shared any of her heart. He gave himself a mental kick. *Which was more important, Kincaid?*

In the parking lot, she removed her arm from his and stopped beside her car. "Where are my keys?" She rummaged in her large purse.

The search took more than a few seconds, as if she needed time to… What? Cullen refrained from probing.

Finally, keys in hand, she looked up.

The dark flecks around her pupils seemed to glow. Her porcelain skin was tinged with ink. He had to stop himself from leaning down and kissing her. "What's running through your mind?"

"I want to accept Jesus as my Savior and be baptized."

He almost kicked his heels together. Instead, he hugged her. "My neighbors have a pool. I'm sure they won't mind if we use it."

While his soul rejoiced, his heart beat a rapid-fire rhythm in his chest. He couldn't help himself and picked up Anna and twirled her around.

Chapter 24

Still basking in the euphoric glow of her Christian walk, Anna entered FARA, collected her badge and coat and almost giggled. Cullen and his insistence she choose a code word had added to her feelings of security. She knew she could trust Jesus's promises of forgiveness and grace and rely on Cullen for her physical well-being. It was reassuring to have someone in her corner. During their conversations yesterday, she'd noted his change in attitude, and appreciated that he hadn't tried to control her life, physical or spiritual.

Thirty minutes into Anna's shift, the lab door opened and a woman wearing the ever-present navy-blue coat gestured for Georgina Jones to approach. They whispered, then the supervisor hurried to Anna.

"Dr. Ubanks needs your assistance."

Although Anna recognized the woman as one she'd eavesdropped on in the cafeteria, she closed the computer file she worked on and calmly walked to the door.

Without a word, Dr. Ubanks led Anna to an elevator and headed down to sub-level four. They wove through the maze of halls to a lab designated as 'Advanced Cas-9'. The hairs on the back of Anna's neck prickled. Cas-9 and CRISPR were interconnected.

"Ms. Jones has praised your ability to correctly decipher handwritten notes. I have several scripts for you to input."

Anna followed Ubanks to the back of the lab where computers lined a counter which faced the door. While entering the data which Anna tried desperately to memorize, commotion at the front drew her attention. Dr. Hays walked in sans wheelchair. He had a slight limp and used a cane.

Hmm. The treatment worked. Anna continued her assignment but kept an eye on Hays. If he came anywhere near her, she'd ask him about his physical improvement. He conversed with Dr. Ubanks as they strode past counters where technicians gazed through microscopes or jotted notes. When the scientists reached the last counter, Dr. Hays spied Anna and his mouth gaped.

She smiled at him but he didn't respond in kind.

He turned to Ubanks and conversed in German. Anna typed away but focused on their every word.

Hays: What is she doing here? She was in my training class a few weeks ago when I was confined to a wheelchair, before the treatments took effect.

Ubanks: How was I supposed to know that? We're so short-staffed I nabbed the first person recommended to me.

Hays: I'll have to talk to her since she's seen me.

Ubanks: Fine. Don't mention the nature of your recovery.

Hays: I won't. I'm not a fool.

A deep red flush highlighted his red hair as Hays approached Anna. "Good morning, young lady. I knew you'd pass the test."

"Good to see you out of your wheelchair, Dr. Hays. Your legs weren't paralyzed. What kind of miracle cure or treatment"—she chose that word with care—"did you receive?"

If possible, his flush intensified. Anna wasn't sure if it was the result of embarrassment or anger. "Um, a new medication from my doctor. I have to go." He pivoted and without another word to Ubanks, stormed out of the lab.

Anna turned the page in the notebook and began typing again, ignoring Ubanks's glare. She wanted to question the scientist, but now might not be a good time. Still working at noon, Anna was escorted to the cafeteria where she sat with Danny. The enticing aromas were a welcome change from the antiseptic odors in the labs.

"Why did a green coat bring you to lunch?"

Anna explained her situation. "This assignment is much more interesting. I hope it becomes permanent."

"Probably not. Maroon coats never work in sub-level four. Your case is an exception, I assure you."

"Then I'll considerate it a privilege. But why is four off limits to us?"

Hunkering over his plate, he looked around as if checking on anyone eavesdropping. "That's where the secret labs are. You know, where they conduct experiments on…" He straightened. "I better not say anymore."

Anna couldn't tell if he was serious or kidding. Although her insides quivered with excitement, she remained calm. "Interesting." She pushed aside her tray. "If ever you want to share more about four, I'll be a receptive listener."

Mr. Green Coat came to escort her back.

"See you later, Danny." Anna returned to the lab and completed the data entry just before three.

"Excellent job, Ms. Knight. I might have to call on you again." Dr. Ubanks pointed to the man who'd escorted Anna. "Andrew will take you to your lab."

Anna massaged her stiff neck muscles and smiled at Andrew as they entered the elevator.

The short, thin man punched in the floor code and smirked. "Don't think for a minute you're going to get my job. I can't believe Dr. Ubanks invited you to four."

No help forthcoming from Andrew, that was certain. Anna thanked him as she entered her usual domain, then shook her head. The staff shortage situation might prove beneficial to her. She reported back to Georgina who suggested the invitation to four was a one-off.

Undeterred, Anna watched the clock while stowing supplies, eager to get home and prepare for the July 4th celebrations. The thought she might see Cullen there never crossed her mind. At least not more than once. Or twice.

~

Dressed in denim cut-offs and a yellow T-shirt, Anna moseyed down to Port Townsend's waterfront. She'd missed the evening parade, but vendors lined the route along Water Street. Red, white, and blue bunting decorated storefronts, and many people waved flags or sported outrageous items of clothing in the tricolors.

Anna purchased three strands of beads to show her

patriotism. She had a perfectly good shirt at home which depicted the American flag, but didn't even think to wear it. Too concerned about a possible meeting with Cullen.

Munching on buttery popcorn, she strolled eastward to where the local high school band played a variety of upbeat music. Enterprising citizens had lawn chairs strategically placed to view the fireworks display which wouldn't begin until sunset, about nine fifteen. Anna casually studied each group of people. Even seated, Cullen would be easy to spot, but her search proved unsuccessful.

The roar of a motorbike drew her attention to a small parking area nearby. She deposited her empty popcorn bag in a trashcan and walked toward the lot. Sure enough, Cullen dismounted and removed his helmet. Anna's heart danced a two-step and she smiled. However, her joy dissipated when Cullen turned to a woman who handed him her helmet. He stowed both on the back of the bike, and although his companion was tall, he leaned over and spoke to her. Anna couldn't hear what he said, but the caring expression on his face yelled all she needed to know.

Her leaden feet wouldn't move. She stared at the pair, willing the ocean to sweep over the rocky beach and swallow her. Then Cullen noticed Anna. She wasn't sure what she expected him to do, but placing one hand on the brunette's shoulders and waving with the other was not on her list.

Disappointment propelled her muscles. She ran back the way she'd come, turned up Tyler Street and headed toward the long flight of stairs that led to Uptown where she'd parked her car. However, she stopped at the fountain to catch her breath. Used to analyzing her emotions and reactions, she set her mind in gear. Why did she flee? Cullen mentioned he'd be attending the celebration, but he didn't turn the statement into a date with her. How was he to know she cared for him? She'd never given him any indication she admired him. Liked him. *Admit it, Annika, you overreacted to seeing him with a beautiful woman because Lexie was right. You do have romantic inclinations.*

In no mood to watch fireworks when she battled explosions within her heart and mind, she trailed her fingers through the cold water splashing into the pool in an effort to lower her level of turmoil. The endeavor failed. She turned to leave, but bumped into a person walking past. Anna said, "Sorry. I wasn't—" Glancing up, her apology stuck in her throat.

The middle-aged woman squinted at her then halted.

They stared at each other.

Anna's hair flowed loose about her shoulders. Although the woman's blonde hair formed a perfect chignon, a white streak ran from her forehead and draped around to be caught at the back. But that was the least of Anna's concerns.

On the verge of a panic attack, she backed away and almost tripped over a small rock. No. No. This person's hairstyle might be a carbon copy of Claire's, but her facial features resembled Anna's, more than enough to be a fluke of nature.

Before she could react, Cullen hurried toward her and called out, "Anna, wait."

Torn between meeting her look-alike and exposing

her…jealousy, Anna chose neither and vaulted halfway up the steps. She glanced over her shoulder. The woman still stared after her and the brunette had joined Cullen.

Anna drove home as the first volley of fireworks whistled and boomed over the ocean. She parked in her driveway and remained in the car. How could her soul be filled with joy but her heart feel as if it were packed with cement?

Chapter 25

Armed with the belief the mystery woman Anna bumped into at the fountain and the one who stared at Clara's portrait at FARA were one and the same, she looked for every opportunity to discover her identify. No luck until Anna visited the cafeteria with Danny. Seated at a table to Anna's right, Judy Coates held a conversation with Anna's quarry.

"Hey, Danny. Do you know the person Judy's talking to?"

Munching on a crispy bread roll, he shook his head.

"This is the first time I've seen Judy since orientation. Excuse me." Anna casually approached the pair who spoke in German. "Sorry to interrupt, Ms. Coates."

They stopped talking and glanced up at Anna.

"Thank you for preparing us to work here, Judy." Anna focused on the other woman's nametag. Terri Ward. "I really like my job and hope to pass my probationary period."

Terri looked anywhere but at Anna. Judy only nodded.

Smiling to herself, Anna returned to her meal and couldn't help but notice the women look her way and lean toward each other as they talked. On the downside, Terri now knew Anna's name too. Couldn't be avoided. Judy would have told her anyway.

The rest of Anna's day passed without incident. Or sojourns to other labs. On the way home, she longed to call Cullen and ask him to research Terri Ward, but the sight of his familiarity with the brunette sat too fresh in her mind. She ate a bland meal, then retreated to her studio. Although the evening light was not ideal, she did slap colors on the canvas that eventually took on an abstract vibe of a turbulent ocean and passionate sky. She stepped back and viewed the painting which depicted her frame of mind exactly.

After cleaning up the studio and showering, Anna wrote in her journal. She sent a brief text to Cullen, as promised, and decided to try her hand at research. There must be public records of Terri Ward, a scientist and Washington State resident.

Anna located information on three people by that name. One resided in Oklahoma, one in Hawaii who spelled her name *Terry*, and the third in Washington, but the photograph didn't resemble Terri and she worked at a local grocery store. Not discouraged yet, Anna discovered Terri or Terry could be a derivation of Theresa. The name jogged a memory.

Aha. Cullen's research revealed Clara and Hugo had a daughter named Therese. Anna located the family timeline he'd made and noted he'd added the three children born to Clara and Hugo in Germany. He also included other pertinent data—dates the boys died, Therese immigrated to the USA in 1969, and her husband's name, Cecil Edwards.

Born in 1937, Therese would now be 85.

However... Anna leaned back in her chair and rocked. However, if Therese inherited her parents' modified genes, or if hers had been altered, she could be the Terri Ward from FARA.

Anna wrote on a sheet of scrap paper. Therese Edwards. Terri Ward. Then she chuckled. "Oh, how clever. Terri, nickname for Therese or Theresa. Ward from Edwards." Besides having similar facial features and blonde hair with a distinctive white streak, the names indicated to Anna the scientist was her sister.

What should she do with this information? Tell Cullen for sure at the next Wednesday Bible study and try to meet Terri to discuss the consequences of their parents' actions.

In spite of her discovery, Anna slept well and entered FARA eager to initiate a meeting with Terri. Having lunch at the same time as the previous day didn't prove fruitful. She asked Danny if he knew Ms. Ward.

"No, sorry. Why do you ask?"

With her recent commitment to live as a follower of Christ still fresh, Anna answered truthfully. "She looks like someone from my past."

"Interesting." He sliced into his juicy steak. "I know I haven't been here much longer than you, but one thing I've learned is don't show curiosity in the higher-ups, especially while on probation. One chap who trained with me asked too many questions and was fired after two weeks."

Anna savored the creamy parmesan-coated pasta as she inhaled the sharp aroma. "Thanks for the advice." But she would take advantage of every opportunity to meet Terri.

Throughout the afternoon, Anna made several trips to different labs on level two. Toward the end of her shift, she caught sight of a blonde woman in a navy-blue lab coat who seemed to be following her. Could it be Terri? When Anna turned and attempted to approach the person, she disappeared through a door to which Anna had no access. The woman walked with difficulty and clutched her right side as if in pain. If Terri was following her, maybe Anna would get the opportunity to meet.

Toting her new Bible to the evening study, Anna sat beside Lexie and eagerly flipped through the crisp pages to Ephesians. Tom concluded his lesson on the Armor of God, focusing on the helmet of salvation and the sword of the Spirit. She'd purposedly bought a Bible with a concordance so she could look up other scriptures to help her understand the wealth of information Tom shared.

Cullen said the closing prayer then occupied the seat Lexi had vacated. "Thanks for texting me each evening."

He hesitated as if he had more to say, but she interrupted because she didn't want to address their last meeting. "I discovered something interesting." She told him all she knew about Terri Ward.

"I agree with your assumptions. She might indeed be Clara's daughter, Therese. What are you going to do next?"

"I want to meet her."

"At FARA? I don't recommend that. The place is so big you could get—"

"You think she will kidnap me, or worse." Standing, she tucked her Bible under her arm.

Cullen stood too, towering over her. "Please quit now. After all, you know your parents are Clara and Hugo and their genes were manipulated. Can we go someplace private to talk?"

"No. I have another painting to complete." *And I don't want to succumb to your dark eyes piercing right through me.*

He set his hands on his hips. "Right. Lexie told me about the exhibition. I'll stop by."

"Good. See you then. And I'll let you know when I make contact with Terri."

Shrugging and pursing his lips, he walked away.

Anna spied Lexie across the courtyard and beckoned her. "I'll have three paintings for the show. How about you?"

"Same here. But ladybug, what's with you and Cullen? You treated him as if he had a communicable disease."

Her turn to shrug. "Nothing. He's being bossy again."

"Too bad. I thought you and he might hit it off."

Anna turned before Lexie could see her frown. Itching to ask about the tall brunette but dreading the answer, she only said, "Until Saturday."

The next day, Dr. Ubanks summoned Anna to her lab again. Andrew escorted her and throughout her time there, kept glancing her way. She suspected he resented her presence and ignored him. At the end of the day as he walked with her to the elevator on sub-level four, Anna spied Terri enter a door halfway down the hall. She stopped, turned to Andrew and smiled. "Do you know Terri Ward?"

"Yes."

"What does she do here?"

"She's one of the lead scientists in...can't say anymore."

"Do you know her well?"

"Why?"

"I've seen her a few times and she seems to be moving slower."

Andrew folded his arms across his narrow chest. The same height as Anna, he raised his chin as if to appear taller. "Nosy little probie, aren't you. What's my information worth?"

"Excuse me?" Anna edged closer to the elevator to avoid his garlic breath.

"Have dinner with me tonight and I'll tell you anything you want to know." He quirked his eyebrows at her.

"Thanks, but I have a previous engagement."

Another employee wearing a navy-blue lab coat approached. The doors dinged open, and he entered the elevator with Anna and Andrew. *Thank You, Lord.* No matter what information her escort could share, she did not want to be alone with the smarmy guy in a confined space or on a...date.

After cleaning up the kitchen that evening, Anna jotted updates in her journal, then created one more picture for the exhibition. Sticking with the abstract format, she chose colors that represented the Pacific Northwest's iconic scenery. Greens for the forests, purple and white for the snow-capped Olympic Mountains, and blues for the ocean. Close to midnight, she stepped back from the easel and sighed. Not bad. She set the other two completed canvases beside the latest and compared all three. Other than the style, they were very different. She nibbled on a fingernail. Each one represented an emotional phase she experienced at the time.

Anna always titled her work. She scrawled her signature in black paint on each canvas, then spent time processing the subject matter. Aha. To the first abstract ocean scene, she added *Searching*. The turbulent scene she named *Anxiety*. And she called her last one *Grace*.

Chapter 26

The text Cullen received from his newest client pleased him no end. Referred by Jerome Jennings, the man had asked Cullen to locate his estranged brother. Five hours of research produced results. Cullen prayed the reunion would ease their differences so they could both attend their father's funeral and rebuild their bond.

Cullen documented the case for his files, then visited Jerome's office to receive his payment. Years ago, he'd overcome the awkwardness he felt for earning money using his tech skills. The work enabled him to help people, and he had time to preach and teach. All in all, a perfect setup.

However, no matter the joy he received from a satisfactory conclusion to a case, Anna was never far from his mind. Each evening, he anxiously awaited her text. He persisted, in his mind at least, in wanting her to quit, but knew he had to tread lightly when corresponding with her and not let his desire slip out. She had to know he was conscious of his overbearing manner and did not want to provide her any more ammunition to shun him.

Although they'd talked after the Wednesday night Bible study, he'd almost been frostbitten by her icy attitude. Maybe when he visited her art institute the next day, he could ask for a few minutes alone and find out what he'd done wrong.

While preparing for Sunday's lesson in Sequim, his phone buzzed, and his heart sank when the call indicated Hauser Security. "Hello."

"Mr. Kincaid, there's been a breach at the Bainbridge Island property. Our security guard apprehended the perpetrator."

"How did he get in?"

"*She* used the alarm code."

She? "Who?"

"Trish Thomas. She works for the company."

Not what Cullen expected. Sullen Ken Fredrich, yes, but not jovial Trish. "I'll be there as soon as possible." He ended the call, mounted his Harley, and headed to the island.

Dressed in black sweats and T-shirt, Trish sat at the kitchen table, nursing a glass of water in spite of the handcuffs. She scowled at Cullen when he entered the room.

Henry, the plump, young security guard, had met Cullen at the front door and related what had happened. Although Trish shut off the alarm with the code, the cameras in the house tracked her movements which looked suspicions to the monitoring personnel. They sent Henry to investigate, and then called Cullen.

"What were you looking for, Trish?" Cullen sat in the chair opposite her.

"I don't have to talk to you."

"You don't, but you will be arrested so you'd better get used to…talking."

Maybe Henry hadn't explained the seriousness of

her situation. Her face paled. "Jail?"

"For breaking and entering. You—"

"I didn't break in. I used the code."

Henry chuckled. "Makes no difference."

"Come on, Trish." Cullen softened his tone. "Help yourself by cooperating. What were you after?"

Her gaze shot from Cullen to Henry to her wrists. "I...I can't. She's scary. Threatened me."

"Who? The authorities can keep you safe."

Trish shook her head vigorously. "She paid me to take documents from a safe."

"You broke in before and searched the office, didn't you?"

Another scowl. "No. She did."

"Interesting. Why'd you agree to her request."

"I, um, have debts. Gambling. She's gonna kill me." Trish hung her head. "That's all I'm saying. I want a lawyer."

Easing out of the chair, Cullen motioned for Henry to follow him to the hall. "Can you take her in?"

"No. I only have the authority to apprehend a possible suspect. I'll notify headquarters to call the cops."

"Fine. I'll leave her in your capable hands."

Henry's chubby face pinked. "Thanks. I'll set the alarm when I close up."

By the time Cullen arrived back in Port Townsend, he was starving and stopped by Tom's restaurant for a meal. For once, the owner had time to sit with Cullen in the courtyard.

"The line-cook I hired has turned out to be a good chef. Gives me time to hang up my apron occasionally. How are you, my brother?"

"My day started out great, but I just returned from Anna's house on the island. A break-in."

"Anything taken?"

Cullen shook his head. "How much has Lexie told you about Anna's situation?"

"Only that she inherited the house, some money. You've helped her with research into her parents' history, and she's working a temp job this summer."

Cullen chewed on a bread stick. Lexie had kept Anna's secret. "That's the gist."

Setting his elbows on the table, Tom eyed is guest. "What are you not telling me?"

That discussion could take all night, but Cullen focused on the issue pressing on his heart. "I had thought Anna and I, you know, were getting close. And I, um, I…"

"Just say it, bro."

"I think I'm falling in love with her, but lately she's treated me like I'm a dog with the mange. Is Lexie here? She can help me approach Anna."

"No. She's preparing for the exhibition tomorrow, but I know what she'd say. Have you told Anna how you feel?"

Again, Cullen shook his head.

"That's your first step. Your next action will depend on how she responds to your declaration."

Taking another bite of the bread stick, Cullen hiked a shoulder. "Now I have to find the courage to say those laden words."

Tom stood and slapped Cullen on the shoulder. "You can do it. Go with God." He disappeared into the restaurant.

Cullen concluded his meal and considering the

possibility Anna might also be busy at the art institute, he texted her details about the break-in instead of paying her a visit.

But she called immediately. "Thank you for taking care of the situation for me. The sooner I sell that house the better. I think the person who broke in the first time and paid Trish might be Terri Ward from FARA. Who else would know about documents in a safe?"

"You're right. Do you have anything to share about your day at FARA?"

"No." The iciness in her voice chilled Cullen's ear.

"Be careful. I'll see you tomorrow." He bowed his head. "Father God, please give me the words I need to convince Anna to leave FARA and to tell her I love her." He slipped his phone into his pocket. Had he ended the call before he'd voiced the prayer?

Chapter 27

Students buzzed around the lobby, checking on their projects, making sure each painting was displayed perfectly. Anna reveled in the excited conversations. She and Lexie had rented the space for this their second, and hopefully, annual art exhibition. Maybe next year they would own the whole building.

A shiver slithered down Anna's spine. Obviously, her inheritance would benefit the institute, but she hadn't yet decided if she wanted to keep money earned by performing illegal and unethical medical procedures.

Lexie maneuvered through the throng and tapped Anna's shoulder. "All looks good."

"Thanks to you. Sorry I didn't help much this year."

"No problem. The students did most of the work." Hands on her hips, Lexie surveyed the exhibits. "Look at their paintings. I'm proud of them. And you, ladybug. Three canvases in spite of your job. They are certainly interesting. How do you like the new style?"

"Getting more comfortable with abstract." Not wanting to discuss her situation, Anna glanced at the large clock above the glass doors. "Almost time."

Lexie climbed a few of the steps on the curved staircase and whistled. The students hushed.

"Congratulations to everyone. Remember, even if your works don't sell today, you are all a success." She gestured with her arms wide. "Anna, open the doors."

A few people entered, mostly relatives of the students, but as the day wore on, more and more locals and tourists viewed the works, purchased many, and left complimentary remarks in the guest book.

At noon, as Anna headed to a classroom set aside for breaks, Terri Ward stepped over the threshold. Anna peeked around a large canvas and watched the women. She strolled among the exhibits, stopped by Anna's entry titled *Anxiety,* then turned and surveyed the room.

Lexie spotted her. "Welcome to our second annual art exhibition. I'm Lexie, one of the partners. Do you need any help?"

"I'm overwhelmed by all the quality paintings. The posters around town advertise the work is done by students."

"Students, past and present, and the staff. We're proud of their accomplishments."

Terri adjusted her sunhat which, Anna noted, covered the white streak in her hair. "My name's Terri. I'd like to meet Anna Knight. One of her paintings intrigues me."

"Certainly." Lexie spied Anna still partially concealed and beckoned her. "You have a fan. This is Terri. Oh, my husband's here. Excuse me." She met Tom as he entered the crowded lobby.

Anna straightened her shoulders and smiled. "Hello, Terri."

"So, Miss Knight, I see you have a passion for art." The woman, about five-foot-four, a couple of inches shorter than Anna, and wearing tinted glasses, tilted her head. "Why then do you want to work at FARA?"

"I think you know why."

Terri nodded. "This is not the place to discuss our heritage. Can you come to my home later this afternoon?"

Provided with the opportunity to question her *sister*, Anna swallowed the anxiety critters inching up her throat. "Yes. We close at four. I can come about five or five thirty."

"Great." Terri fished in her purse and withdrew a slip of paper which she handed to Anna. "This is my address. Let's say five thirty. Ooh. My eyes." She removed her glasses and rubbed her left eye. She blinked and put her glasses back on, but not before Anna noted a yellow tinge to the whites of her eyes.

"I'll see you then." Anna gestured to the hive of activity around her. "I need to circulate. Goodbye."

Terri massaged her right side as she left the building. Anna retreated to the breakroom and collapsed into a chair. No amount of calming breaths could subdue the roiling in her stomach. Anxiety or excitement? She didn't care at this point. She would finally have the answers she needed to chart the course of her life.

One of the students had left the crusts of a tuna fish sandwich on a napkin. Anna had never been a fan and wrinkled her nose as she delivered the offending odor to the trash.

Emerging from the classroom, she stopped in her tracks. Cullen and Lexie stood across the room, chatting and laughing. Not so unusual, except for the brunette who joined in the fun. *How could you Lex? First, you hint that Cullen and I would make a good pair, and now you're joking with his girlfriend.*

Anna wanted to, no, needed to tell Cullen about her meeting with Terri, but no way did she intend to speak to him with brunette in tow. Instead, she answered a customer's question then busied herself with straightening canvases on easels, but a few minutes later, Cullen tapped her shoulder.

"What a great turnout. Lexie tells me most of the paintings have been sold."

A smile fixed on her face, Anna turned to be greeted by Cullen with his arm around the tall, beautiful, brunette. "Yes." She cleared her throat. "Even two of my attempts at abstracts."

"Where are my manners? Anna, this is Erin, my youngest sister."

Sister? Of course. Up close, Anna noticed the resemblance. Same eyes, same dark, wavy hair and face shape. She extended her hand. "Hi, Erin. Nice to meet you." Indeed. She wasn't quite sure what her heart was doing but she covered it with one hand.

"Cullen has spoken about you so much. I'm glad we finally met."

Curious about what Cullen had told his siter, Anna fought the desire to inquire. Instead, she asked, "Have you visited Port Townsend before?"

"Several times. Mainly to check up on my big brother's, um, prospects." Erin blushed as she poked him in the ribs. "However, my college roommate in Poulsbo recently gave birth to premature twins, and I've spent my time helping her and keeping an eye on Cullen."

"Which reminds me, sis, we need to leave soon."

"Wait, please Cullen. I have information to share."

Anna could have hugged Lexie who gestured for Erin to join her with a group of students.

"I'll be quick. Terri Ward came in earlier. She invited me to her house."

He frowned and hovered over her. "You're not going, are you? Remember, she's probably behind the attempted thefts from your mother's office."

Stepping backward, Anna replied, "I haven't forgotten. I'm meeting her at five thirty today."

"Sorry for...encroaching on your space, but I don't think it's a good idea."

"Why not? What can Terri do to me?" She craned her neck to look into his eyes. "And I know she'll have answers to the questions that have gnawed at me since I began this pursuit into my parents' past."

"I can see you're determined. Give me her address, please."

Anna held out the piece of paper and he entered the details into his phone.

"Be careful. Keep your phone with you and text me when you get home again. I'm spending the night with Erin in Poulsbo, but I can come back if you need me." His dark eyes raked her face. "Please."

"I will." As difficult as it was to admit, she did need Cullen. Not just today.

Erin joined him. "Time to go."

"I know." He brushed a strand of hair off Anna's forehead. "I'll be teaching in Sequim tomorrow. Can you come?"

"I'd like to. Text me the address."

He nodded and ushed Erin out the door.

Anna sighed and leaned against the wall. Sister. If only she'd known that last week. She folded her arms across her middle, not to quieten the anxiety bugs, but to contain the effervescing excitement. Cullen did not have a girlfriend and Anna would see him tomorrow, listen to him sing and teach. She pursed her lips. Yes, now she could admit she was falling in love with him.

Heat rose up her neck as Lexie strolled over.

"I do believe our exhibition has been a success. Every student sold at least one offering, we have loads of positive comments in the guest book, and several people have signed up for classes in the fall."

"Wonderful. This is your success, Lex. I can't wait to get back to our institute." Anna chose not to tell Lexie about her meeting later, but added, "I think I'll soon be ready to quit my other job."

"Hey, ladybug, I know this whole ordeal has been messy, but through it all, you found the courage to accept Jesus as your Savior and you'll do the right thing concerning your parents."

The next hour rushed by while the students and staff removed all vestiges of the exhibition from the lobby.

Anna checked her watch. Five fifteen.

Lexie asked, "Want to join me at the restaurant for a celebratory meal?"

"Not this evening, thanks. I'm meeting...someone from FARA. I think she'll be able to help me."

"I understand. Keep safe, my friend." With a wave, Lexie disappeared into a classroom.

Stepping onto the sidewalk, Anna straightened her shoulders. She told Lexie no lies. Except to identify the *someone* as Terri Ward, her eighty-five-year-old sister.

Chapter 28

The Victorian house on Lincoln Street, set back off the road and surrounded by Douglas firs and colorful gardens, harked back to Port Townsend's prosperous history. Anna climbed the steps to the wrap-around porch.

Lacy curtains in the glass panel of the door twitched. Terri opened the door before Anna knocked. "Come in. We have lots to talk about."

Without the tinted glasses, Anna confirmed Terri's eyes were definitely jaundiced. "Thanks for this opportunity." Her voice quavered. She sucked in a breath and surveyed the interior. Floral wallpaper, a curved wooden staircase, gleaming hardwood floors. Hints of honeysuckle emanated from a bowl of potpourri on the entry table flanked by two straight-backed chairs. An old-fashioned telephone jostled for space on the table.

"I know you want answers. Follow me to the basement." Wearing a black dress and black ankle boots, Terri led the way down the hall to a door midway along the wall.

They descended the stairs to a bright basement fitted out with lab equipment, sinks, tables, and a slew of microscopes on a counter abutting a sitting area.

In spite of her excitement, Anna's familiar apprehension began to churn in her gut. She tried to ignore it and sat on the sofa where Terri directed and set her purse beside her. With Cullen's advice in mind, she kept her cell phone in the pocket of her baggy, cream-colored linen pants.

"I prepared snacks. Help yourself while I pour the lemonade." Her host pointed to the coffee table where magazines were strewn beside plates of cookies and finger sandwiches and turned to a trolley behind her.

Famished, Anna selected one of each treat onto her plate. She sniffed the little sandwich. Mmm. Cilantro accompanied the cucumber slices. Before she leaned back against the soft cushions, words in a magazine's cover headline caught her attention. *Nachwelt Foundation Receives Anonymous Multi-Million Dollar Gift.* Her mother's legacy? Not sure Terri knew about their parents' finances, she pointed to the glossy publication. "What do you know about the Nachwelt Foundation and this money?"

Terri set two glasses of lemonade on coasters then piled snacks onto her plate. She sipped her drink. "The foundation funds many research facilities, but FARA is their main focus."

"Figures," Anna muttered.

"What?"

Shrugging, Anna took a bit of a shortbread cookie.

"I won't keep you in suspense. I am Clara and Hugo's daughter, and yes, they changed their names to Claire and Hugh, our parents." Terri held up her glass and saluted Anna. "Here's to us, sis."

Fingers gripping her glass, Anna didn't know

whether to laugh or cry. She set her plate down before she dumped the contents into her lap. "I thought as much, but..." Now the truth had been disclosed, Anna had a hard time absorbing the facts. Her parents had undergone genetic modifications. But what about her?

Thirsty beyond the norm, she drained her glass. "I have other questions."

"I know you do, but first, I'll pour more lemonade for us." Terri took their glasses to the trolley and refilled them.

Anna tried to form her questions, but her tongue seemed to trip over her teeth. She gave up and finished another sandwich, washing it down with the last of her second glass of lemonade. She attempted to set the glass on the table, but her muscles wouldn't cooperate. Terri took the glass and plate from her and chatted non-stop.

Although Anna couldn't move, she understood everything Terri said.

"For the longest time, I didn't know what our parents had done. Even when I suspected something was amiss, they lied to me. But I eventually got the truth out of them. By the time my eldest brother and my twin and I were born, our parents had already worked for Das Institut for several years. That is where they received their first gene manipulation."

Anna forced her head to turn toward the lab area where Terri bustled around as if intent on a breakthrough experiment.

"They didn't try any alterations to our genes until we were toddlers. Each one of us received a different treatment. Obviously, my brothers' interventions weren't as successful as mine." Terri grabbed her right side. "That is, until now."

Jaundiced eyes, pain. Possible liver failure. But Anna's questions backlogged in her brain.

"As an adult in Germany, I didn't want any association with our parents, so I moved out of Munich. However, science was in my blood." She chuckled, a perverse sound considering the circumstances. "I studied hard at university and later, applied to work on my doctorate degree in genetics in the USA. When FARA advertised their need for scientists with my qualifications, I snapped at the chance."

Terri wheeled a cart over to Anna and pulled on latex gloves. She applied a torniquet to Anna's upper left arm

What are you doing? Anna's eyes must have expressed the question.

"Not to worry. I need to see if your blood is compatible with mine." She used an alcohol swab on the bend in Anna's elbow then inserted a needle and withdrew a vial of blood. Taking the cart with her, Terri disappeared behind a screen but kept up the flow of her informative monologue.

"I didn't know Mama and Papa had also immigrated. Imagine my surprise when I walked into the FARA facility where the giant portrait of Clara gazed down on me. It didn't take long to discover Frank Ahn had left Das Institut in Berlin, established FARA near Munich, but transferred his company to Seattle. Two months ago, I learned my mother, known as Claire Taylor, worked there, but by then she was ill in hospital. During my only visit, she hinted at incriminating documents hidden in her home office. Believe me, I searched. And sniveling Trish was arrested."

Confirmation Terri was responsible for the attempted thefts.

"Since you didn't flinch when I revealed we're sisters, I presume you found our parents' original birth certificates."

Other than talking, Terri made little noise behind the screen. Anna couldn't figure out what she was doing then the scientist emerged with a grin on her face.

"Do you know your blood type?"

Anna attempted a shrug.

"It's *O* negative. Just my luck you'd be a universal donor."

What did Terri have planned?

Anna didn't have to wait long. By now she had regained a little muscle control, so when Terri lifted her up and forced her toward another screened area, Anna was able to shuffle her feet.

Kicking the screen aside, Terri sat her guest on a gurney. No matter how much Anna resisted, she was no match for Terri's determination. She gave up and lay down. The woman strapped Anna's arms and wrists to the rails with rubber tubing and used more to wrap around her ankles.

"What…doing?" Anna's voice, thready and weak, caught Terri by surprise.

She shot an angry glance at Anna. "I'd better hurry. The drug is wearing off quicker than I anticipated. No problem. This is the real reason I invited you. I want your blood."

"How?"

Answers were soon evident. Terri inserted an IV needle into a vein in Anna's inner left forearm, attached a long, narrow tube to the luer connector, and secured the tube with tape. She allowed a little blood to collect, then clamped the tube.

Grinning, she reached for a hyperthermic on the cart behind her. "I almost forgot." She introduced the liquid into the injection port of Anna's IV.

"What?"

"Anticoagulant. I've never done this before so I hope I've given you enough. Now, be still." Terri drew an armchair close to the gurney and inserted another IV needle into her right arm. She attached the other end of the tube and secured it with tape. Relaxing in the chair, she opened the clamp on Anna's IV. "Let's see if this works."

From the angle at which Anna lay, she observed her blood trickle through the tube to Terri's arm. None escaped. "How long?"

"I don't know. If I suffer no adverse reaction after fifteen minutes, then I'll continue until my body can't take anymore. I'm anemic and need blood anyway." She let out an enormous sigh as if she'd finally received a desired gift.

Anna's turn to chuckle. Since she'd regained some control over her voice, she had to seek answers she might not live to discover any other way. "Your genes were altered when…young. What about me?"

"I'm hoping yours were manipulated in the embryonic stage. That's why I need your blood."

"Not making sense. How can blood help when altered genes…failing?" Encouraged by her ability to talk more naturally, Anna patted the phone in her right pocket, out of Terri's line of sight.

"I'm going to divulge a little secret. While at

FARA, my team and I developed a drug that can infiltrate cells and alter the host's genes to match the donor's. If our parents performed as I expect, you probably would have lived a long life. Longer than they did and longer than the other FARA scientists who've died recently"

Anna fought against the restraints in vain. But she slipped her right hand into her pocket. To keep Terri distracted and to gain more details, she asked, "You're admitting CRIS...something technology."

"You know about CRISPR? Yup. And my new drug will revolutionize genetics. I gave myself a dose while I was testing your blood."

"But...illegal, unethical."

Terri leaned forward and checked her IV then Anna's. "I feel great and we've been *sharing* for more than fifteen minutes." She grinned. "As to your allegations—sure our procedures are not sanctioned by the medical community. Yet. But don't you think the general public will want to choose characteristics of their babies? Or to slow the aging process? You have no idea what other drugs and procedures FARA is pioneering."

The information Jill shared with Faulkner had been correct. "If my genes were manipulated at conception, then I'll pass the changes onto my children. Right?"

"Annika, my naive sister. Don't worry about your future. Without my intervention, you might have outlived a spouse, as I did, but you won't survive this procedure. Even if you do, you won't leave my house alive. Relax, sleep."

Well, she couldn't pass on her genetic makeup if she was dead. Undeterred, Anna continued probing while she fingered her phone. Although she gained more and more muscle control as the minutes passed, she was now feeling the effects of dramatic blood loss and could barely turn her head. She struggled to speak. "Why do this to me? Surely, I'm not the only offspring of the people involved in FARA's bizarre experiments."

"Because we're related. And proximity. You were at FARA. I noticed your resemblance to Clara and me when we bumped into each other in Port Townsend. I discovered you visited headquarters in Seattle and collected Clara's, rather Claire's personal items. Why? Because you're her daughter. And then I learned you were a trainee at FARA. How convenient for me."

"Will my blood cure your liver failure?"

"Sure hope so. You and I are the first human trials. Only done the procedure on rats and it works most of the time."

Terri's terrifying word wafted over Anna who couldn't keep her eyes open. She drifted in and out of consciousness, until she fell into a deep, dark hole.

~

Blinking against the bright overhead light, Anna frowned. Where was she? Memory slowly returned. Basement. Terri. Blood.

IV needle and restraints still in place, Anna glanced around and listened. No captor. She withdrew the phone from her pocket, moved her legs closer to the rail, and bent her knees. The tubing gave her enough slack to prop the phone on her legs. With a prayer on her lips for cell reception, she tapped in her code then had to fight lethargy and the device's tendency to slide off her legs. Summoning all her strength, she texted Cullen. *New lab coat.* As she entered the void again, Anna

217

heard the distinct ping of a sent message.

Chapter 29

Although Erin protested, Cullen had decided to return home instead of spending the night in Poulsbo. He'd read a news article about Harold Faulkner, a prominent Seattle scientist who'd died of a heart attack and wanted to be available in case Anna needed him.

While waiting at a stoplight in Port Townsend, his phoned dinged. He glanced at the text.

New lab coat.

He pulled into a parking lot, but Anna didn't respond to his reply, nor did she answer his call. Blood on fire with adrenalin and gut churning, he headed to Anna's house. No. She had plans to visit Terri. Cullen remembered her address. He turned on Washington Street, drove up the hill toward Lincoln, and checked house numbers. No. No. Then he spied Anna's vehicle in the driveway of a stately Victorian. He parked on the street and crept toward the porch steps.

He knocked. No noise or movement from inside. He tried the knob. The door opened an inch but wouldn't budge any further. Might be blocked by a heavy object. He pressed his shoulder against the door and pushed. The object must be made of concrete. He put his weight behind the next attempt and the door opened a few more inches. Another push and the blockade scraped the wooden floor. And again, until Cullen could squeeze through the gap.

No subtle entry. He noted the trunk by the door then his gaze swept the foyer, the hall. A movement on the curved staircase caught his attention.

A woman who looked like an older version of Anna descended a half dozen steps. Hands in her pockets, Terri asked, "Who are you?"

"I'm looking for Anna. Her car's out front."

"I forgot about..." She pulled a handgun with suppressor attached from one pocket and aimed it at Cullen. "Go down the hall to the kitchen."

Pale, shaking, blood oozing from a bandage on her arm, Terri posed no threat. Cullen could easily overpower her. "Tell me where Anna is and I'll leave with her."

"No." The woman waved the weapon his direction. "Go to the kitchen, now."

"What if I don't?"

She descended a few more steps. "I'll shoot you, but more important, I won't tell you where Anna is. And if she doesn't get medical help within the next...ten minutes, she'll die."

Hands clenched into fists and jaw muscles rigid, Cullen walked down the hall aware Terri clomped behind him. He knew he could disarm her, but if her threat held any weight, he would put Anna's life at risk. At the kitchen counter, he turned. "I did what you told—"

Crack!

A sharp, hot projectile pierced his thigh. *She shot*

me. He slid down the cabinet to the tiled floor as blood seeped from his wound.

Unfazed, Terri pivoted, opened a door in the hall and disappeared.

He removed his belt and strapped it around his thigh. Although the wound bled, he didn't think the bullet hit the femoral artery. At least he wouldn't bleed to death. He assessed his situation while taking his phone from his T-shirt pocket. How could he discover Anna's location? He called her phone again. No answer and he didn't hear it ring. He did, however, sense a presence above his head and looked up.

Terri shoved a hypodermic into his neck. He grabbed her hand and removed the needle, but as his eyes lost focus, he succumbed to the drug. His body seemed as heavy as the weights at the gym. He was powerless to stop her. She dragged his body to the center island, handcuffed his wrists behind his back, and slapped duct tape over his mouth.

Semi-conscious, Cullen tried to sit up, find his phone. Remove the tape. Call the cops. But his muscles refused to obey his brain. His feeble attempt to kick at the stout metal leg of the island produced little sound. *Please, God. Help us.* His battle to keep his eyes open failed.

He had no idea how long he lay there, coasting between consciousness and sleep. A thud as if someone opened the front door and it bashed into the trunk. As alert as possible, Cullen attempted to sit, but during one of his blackouts, Terri had chained the too-small handcuffs securing his wrists to the leg of the island. He lay on his side surrounded by his blood and shifted his position to better see his captor enter the kitchen.

Not Terri. Anna. No matter what drug he'd been given, nothing could stop his pulse thundering in his ears like a motorbike engine.

"Oh, my darling, Cullen." Anna knelt beside him, gently removed the tape, and ran her smooth hands over his cheeks. "What has she done to you?"

All Cullen heard was *darling*. He gazed at her face so close to his and frowned. "What happened to you?" Face ashen, eyes sunken, hands trembling, and blood oozing from an IV port in her arm. "I'm supposed to rescue you."

Drawing in several breaths, Anna leaned against the cabinets. "Long story. We need to call the police. I can't find my phone."

"I should have notified the authorities after I read your text, but I had to find you first."

"Phone?"

"In my shirt pocket."

Anna tapped the pocket and shook her head. "Sorry."

"You must go for help."

"Okay, but—"

"Sit down, sis." Looming over the counter at them, Terri pointed the gun at Anna's head.

Still groggy, Cullen whispered, "I certainly underestimated her."

"Can I at least help Cullen to sit?"

Terri nodded and walked past them to the table where she sat, the gun aimed their direction.

Aware Anna was in no physical condition to assist him much, he used all his core strength to raise up and maneuver his hips backward to the counter. Pain zapped through his left thigh and the handcuffs cut into his wrists, but he held back the groan.

Anna settled beside him. "She shot you?"

"Yeah, but I've staunched the bleeding."

"Terri, I need first aid supplies from the basement."

"No. I don't care if he dies. In fact, I don't need him." Terri shifted position and pointed the weapon at Cullen.

The concern in Anna's eyes acted as a balm. Cullen smiled. "Anna, my love, I have bad news. Dr. Faulkner had a heart attack and died yesterday."

Apparently weakened by her effort to help him, she rested her head on his shoulder. "That's terrible. Probably FARA had to stop him reporting their illegal practices." She huffed out a heavy sigh. "I don't have the energy to deal with the news. My life is slipping away and I have to tell you something, Cullen. I love you."

He barely heard her sweet words, but replied, "I love you, Annika."

Chapter 30

Fighting to stay conscious, Anna stared at Terri. The woman appeared to have aged in the past few hours. Her facial skin sagged, she often gasped for breath, and she couldn't hold up her head for more than a minute or two.

"I guess my blood's not performing the miracle you wanted."

"I'll take more when I'm rested." She wiggled the gun at Anna.

Anna closed her eyes and relived the exchange she and Cullen had shared. Love, but were their declarations too late?

He nudged her side and whispered, "Tell me what she did."

"Terri drugged the snacks or lemonade she served in the basement. Strapped me to a gurney and began a blood transfusion." Anna related what she could remember from Terri's oration, stopping frequently to draw in air. "FARA has been conducting illegal procedures for a long time." She shrugged. "But I don't know what modifications were made to my genes."

"Is there a way to find out?"

"I don't know. And my *sister's* in no position to

help me."

Cullen turned toward Anna. "How did you get away?"

"I must have slept for quite a while after I texted you. When I awoke, I had the strength to wrestle with the restraints she'd used to tie my wrists. They were flexible enough that I slipped my right hand out, removed the IV tube and clamped it, then untied my left hand, arms, and ankles. The door was locked, but I pushed a table to the wall, broke a window, and climbed out. I was on my way to the neighbors to call the police, but noticed your Jeep and came inside."

"You shouldn't have."

"I know that now, but I had to make sure you were all right."

He grinned. "I'm all right now you're beside me. I wish I could put my arms around you, my love."

"Will you settle for me snuggling close?"

"Yep."

"Until I met you, I didn't know I had empty places in my life. I knew my soul had unfilled holes, and now my soul is whole. But my life, well, Mr. Kincaid, how do you propose filling the holes in my life when we're at Terri's mercy?" Anna gestured toward the woman.

Their captor braced her left arm when the weapon wavered.

"I waited a long time for someone who'd make me whole, too. And since you mentioned the word 'propose', will you marry me?"

Bubbling excitement overtook Anna's anxiety for a moment. "I can't answer that until you hear my concerns." She cleared her throat. "As already discussed, I don't know what changes my parents made to my genes. I might live to be two hundred, I might never get sick."

"I don't care what happens to your body. I'll take you for better or worse and I'll love you forever."

Anna smiled. "And I'll—"

"Your tenderness is making me nauseous." Terri sneered at them. "Good news, bad news, sis."

Interested, Anna straightened.

"FARA has a vault on sub-level five where they house their records. Decades of records. You're curious about your genes? Yours, mine, our parents'? All there. But you won't get to read them." She took careful aim at Anna.

Cullen shifted his body to cover her.

Boom. A shot zapped close to her head.

He slumped on her shoulder.

"Cullen." While anger and dread fought for supremacy in her gut, she raised his head. A trickle of blood danced across his forehead to his cheek. She shook him and received a wink and a brief smile as his chest rose and fell negligibly.

Acting a part. She could participate and cradled his head against her chest. "Why'd you do that, Terri? He's dead."

A moan rose from the woman. She dropped the gun which clattered to the floor then she wilted in the chair, arms dangling at her sides.

Cullen kept up the charade.

Easing his limp body off her, Anna crawled to the table and slid the weapon toward him. "Terri?" Her voice sounded distant and muffled.

No response.

Anna felt for a pulse. Not even a flutter. She

shrugged and looked at Cullen who'd raised his head.

Surrendering to fatigue and relief, she squatted on the floor and covered her ears. Shock waves pounded her eardrums. Aware the close shot affected Cullen's hearing too, she yelled, "I'll look for our phones." Using another chair as leverage, she pulled herself up, staggered down the hall, and spotted the landline phone beside the bowl of potpourri. She'd probably never appreciate the sweet scent of honeysuckle again. "Thank You, Lord." Sinking into a chair, she dialed 9-1-1.

"What's your emergency?"

Anna almost laughed. "Send everyone. My friend's been shot, I need a blood transfusion, and the owner of the house is dead. We need bolt cutters, and maybe a hazmat team. There's blood everywhere, and this woman has a lab in her basement and sensitive medical records of illegal procedures being conducted at the Frank Ahn Research facility."

That about covered it all.

~

In the hospital the next day, Anna sat by Cullen's bed. She'd received a tetanus shot and antibiotics to combat unhygienic equipment Terri might have used, a blood transfusion, and had been discharged. Cullen required surgery to remove the bullet and had to stay another day.

They'd been questioned by every organization imaginable. Local police, Jefferson County Sherriff, later the FBI, CDC, DEA, and a couple of serious, expressionless agents who didn't wear the ubiquitous cap or jacket identifying their group.

Finally, alone after a visit from Tom and Lexie,

Anna took Cullen's hand and kissed the abrasions on his wrist. "Do they hurt?"

"Not anymore. Your kiss has healing powers." He puckered his lips. "Kiss me here and I won't need pain meds ever again."

Anna leaned forward and Cullen slipped his arms around her, drawing her close. She ran her hands over his broad chest, up his neck. Into his messy hair, careful to avoid the stitches closing the gash in his temple caused by Terri's second bullet. The horrific events of the last twenty-four hours dissolved and were replaced by a euphoria Anna hadn't experienced before.

Their uneven breathing accompanied their locked gazes. She'd never kissed an unshaven man and lowered her head, her lips brushing his. He covered her mouth with his and caressed her nape, sending shivers of anticipation down her spine. His prickly stubble tickled her face in the most delightful way. She lost herself in the kiss that seemed to go on forever.

A knock on the door. "Excuse me, Mr. Kincaid, I need to take your vitals."

Anna stepped to the window overlooking the Port Townsend waterfront and plucked at the bandage on her arm. She had an important decision to discuss with Cullen. When the nurse had charted his stats and left, Anna returned to the chair. "I've thought a lot about Mother's legacy. I don't want her money, and I believe her estate might be seized while her activities are investigated."

"Good decision. Are you interested in the records Terri alluded to?"

"The possibility kept me awake last night. Even if I'm allowed access, I don't want to know about my genes. Ironic, in that the quest drove my recent actions." She squinted at him. "Speaking of recent actions. Why did you shield me from Terri's aim?"

Cullen stroked her cheek. "Because I want to protect you. Now and forever. Which reminds me, we have unfinished business. First, I'm truly sorry for trying to control you."

"I liked your interference, um, suggestions at first because I felt secure, cared for. But later, my anxiety took over and overwhelmed me."

"I realize that now, and I promise to relinquish control over every aspect of your life." He cocked his head and a gave her a half-smile. "Except one last time. And I'm sure I'll get my way."

Frowning, Anna straightened. If he didn't look so doggone handsome with his bewhiskered face, mussed hair, and goofy smile, she might have bolted. She set her hands on her hips. "What are you sure I will do?"

"Quit your job at FARA."

She collapsed onto his chest and laughed so hard her stomach hurt. When she caught her breath, she asked, "What's the second item?"

"You didn't answer my question. Will you marry me?"

"Yes, darling, and I hope, no I pray we grow old...*together*. In fact, hold my hands." He clasped them. "Father, God. Please bless our union as we serve You for the rest of our lives."

THE END

Valerie's next novel, *Every Hidden Thing*, is a romantic suspense set in Washington State.

"Now all has been heard; here is the conclusion of the matter: Fear God and keep his commandments, for this is the whole duty of man. For God will bring every deed into judgment, including every hidden thing, whether it is good or evil."
Ecclesiastes 12:13–14 (NIV)

Chapter 1

Tremaine Realty specialized in prime waterfront properties on the Pacific Northwest's Olympic and Kitsap Peninsulas. Instead of showing fancy homes to prospective clients, Joanna Tremaine was more often than not assigned to the property management division of the company. Like today. Not exactly her choice, but at least her folks had given her a job after her event planning business went belly-up, and she was determined to prove worthy of their trust.

The serious GPS voice announced her destination ahead, Nelda Yates's extensive property south of Seabeck on the Hood Canal side of the Kitsap Peninsula. Jo stopped at the open electric gate. *Item number one on the repair list: Fix gate.* She drove up the paved, curved driveway shaded by ancient firs and gawked at the stone mansion appearing through the branches. What a house! But when Jo parked in front of the three-car garage, the neglect became apparent. Cracked windows, peeling paint on the wood trim, weeds forcing their way between pavers.

Purse and briefcase in hand, Jo removed the key from the lock box. The carved oak door swung open into a cathedral-ceilinged foyer. "Wow." Jo pivoted slowly, taking in the grandeur. Eager to begin documenting needed touch-ups and repairs, she sauntered through the massive living room where sunlight poured in through floor-to-ceiling windows, then entered the kitchen at the rear. Her mouth gapped. The room was large enough to accommodate her whole apartment. She dumped her purse and briefcase onto the counter.

iPad ready, she opened the back door. She preferred completing the outdoor phase first and ventured to the weathered barn about one hundred yards from the house. The doors hung like loose teeth. Foul, dank air engulfed her. Decaying animal waste carpeted the ground. She wrinkled her nose and stepped carefully. *Mama, this is why I wear boots.* Jo snickered. She always had to defend her choice of wardrobe to her dainty, immaculate mother.

Jo took a dozen or more photos of the dilapidated barn. She would recommend its removal. Satisfied she'd captured all the outside details, she stepped to the door.

The matted straw to her left rustled.

Rodents? Ugh.

A dog whined and poked his dirty head through the stubble. "You poor thing." Jo leaned over, but he withdrew. "I won't hurt you." She used a rake handle to move the straw and gasped. The mid-sized dog was entwined in a coil of barbed wire. He cowered, making it difficult for Jo to extricate him, but one last twist, and he was free. The pooch, with only minor scrapes, scampered away, scruffy brown tail between his legs.

Jo picked up the wire and frowned. In his struggles, the dog had rumpled a dirty, khaki tarpaulin which partially covered a metal container. In order to read the red lettering, she moved aside the canvas and gulped. DANGER. EXPLOSIVES.

Taking a step backward, she stared at her discovery. Surely the former tenants hadn't left dynamite behind.

Aware she'd have to notify the authorities, Jo lifted the tarpaulin to see what else it might conceal and exposed two more green, metal containers. Each measured about fifteen-by-twelve-by-six inches and had handles on the sides.

Had the renters used the barn to store other hazardous items? Jo noted marks in the dirt floor which could indicate heavy objects had been dragged along. And the path to the—

Strident, angry voices floated into the barn through gaps in the wooden slats.

Jo covered the containers, then peeked out through a large gap and spied two people walking from the tree line at the end of the property toward the barn.

"You didn't have to come. Don't you trust me?" Male.

"No, I don't, Wade." Female. "It was your responsibility to load all the ammo containers."

Not dynamite, but ammunition. Jo headed to the door but stopped when the female continued her harangue in a venomous tone.

"Were you planning on coming back for them later to sell yourself?" She tugged at a pale scarf around her neck.

"No. How could you think that, Rosie? I promise, I just forgot how many containers we had."

Their voices grew louder as they neared Jo's position.

"You've put us all in danger. If they fall into the wrong hands, the whole organization could be jeopardized."

"It's not my fault we had to leave in such a hurry. Besides, who's going to search out here?" Wade stomped ahead of his companion.

Aha. The previous tenants.

"Of all the stupid—"

A cell phone rang. The pair halted, not three yards from Jo. Rosie withdrew a phone from her pocket. "It's Boyd. I'll put it on speaker. Yeah?"

"Keep your voices down." Another male. "I think someone's in the house."

"What?" Rosie and Wade hissed together.

"I just drove past and noticed a vehicle in the driveway. Have you collected the merchandise?"

Jo stared at the tarpaulin. Considering the content of the conversation, she had no doubt that revealing her presence would not be healthy.

"No." Rosie jabbed Wade's shoulder. "We haven't entered the barn yet."

"Get out of there and don't return. I'll wait until the person leaves, then I'll pick up the containers."

Wade grabbed Rosie's arm as she ended the call. "Why did you narc on me to Boyd?"

"Let go, Wade. You're hurting me."

He did not release her. "You heard him. We gotta go."

As the intruders ran across the lawn, Rosie's scarf floated to the ground. She stopped and retrieved it, then the couple disappeared into the woods.

Slumping against the wall, Jo rubbed her forehead. Close call. It seemed obvious their possession of ammo containers was suspicious. After one last peek through the gap, Jo hightailed it back to the house and made sure all the doors were locked. She didn't want a surprise visit from Boyd.

Hand shaking, Jo withdrew her phone from her pocket and called the Kitsap County Sheriff's Office. A deputy in the area would arrive as soon as she tended to a minor fender-bender. To calm her jittery insides, Jo sat in the bay window seat in the kitchen and sipped from her water bottle. Her gaze wandered around the room and she fantasized about changes she'd make. Replace the gaudy backsplash with neutral-colored tiles. Stainless steel appliances instead of black. She sighed. Rented apartments were all she could afford for now.

Bravado restored, Jo returned to her task and photographed and itemized needed repairs of the downstairs rooms. Patch up a couple of scrapes and paint the walls, change out mismatched light fixtures. Other than a thorough cleaning, not much else required attention.

However, the upstairs rooms were a disaster. Jo vowed to never rent out any home she might acquire in the future. Empty cardboard boxes and odd bits of furniture littered the bedrooms. Wade and Rosie must have packed up in a hurry, but that didn't account for stained carpets, holes in the sheetrock, or chipped bathroom tiles. Wade would not be getting his security deposit returned, for sure. No wonder Nelda hired Tremaine Realty to oversee repairs before listing the property. The previous company certainly failed in their responsibilities, especially in vetting the last tenants.

In the smallest bedroom, Jo found no damage at all. She opened the closet and other than a missing lightbulb, all seemed in good order. In her limited experience, she'd noted that if tenants left anything behind it was usually something on the top shelf in a closet. At nearly six-feet tall, Jo had no need to stand on tiptoe to reach a shoebox stashed way back against the wall. Expecting to find shoes insides, she was surprised at the assortment of little toys. The kind that might be included in a child's meal from a fast food restaurant. Probably not of any value, but she took the box and would later contact the tenants to see if they wanted it.

After a half-hour of documenting the damage, Jo returned to the kitchen and set the shoebox with her personal items. Next on her list—the gardens. She checked the plantings around the front deck. Weed removal, add mulch and colorful perennials. Taking photos as she walked, she wandered down the driveway and noted landscape problems, especially the pruning or removal of rogue blackberry vines that dominated a hedge of rhododendrons. Overhanging fir tree branches needed trimming, and the vast lawn had to be mowed and edged. She added the disconnected and lopsided electric gate.

Spying a piece of trash in the shrubs, she squeezed between the thick bushes and nabbed the plastic bag. Footsteps crunched on the driveway. Wade or Rosie? Jo peeked through the leaves. Neither. A tall, muscular man walked down the middle of the drive, peering ahead.

Jo blew out a breath and stepped forward. "Can I help you?"

The man halted, hand to his chest. "You startled me." He blew out a breath. "Good morning. I live in the area and I'm curious. Are you the new tenant?"

They were too far from the house for him to see the magnetic advertisement sign on her SUV. Jo extricated herself from the branches and extended her hand. "Jo Tremaine from Tremaine Realty."

"Um, Gerald. Gerry." He shook her hand then pointed over his shoulder. "Is the house for sale? Will you be the listing agent?"

"As soon as we have it in tiptop shape."

"Great. I'm glad you're here. The unkempt yard is an eyesore." The guy's dark brown eyes were in sharp contrast to his sandy-colored hair.

"We'll soon have it under control."

"I'll pass the word that the property will be on the market." He cocked his head. "You're taking pictures?"

"Yes." Jo held up her iPad. "To document damage and areas in need of attention."

He rubbed his chin. "Did the tenants leave a mess?"

Strange question. "You could say that." He didn't need any more details. "I have a lot to do. Nice to meet you, Gerry."

"Same here. Sorry for taking up your time. Do you have a card so I can refer prospective clients?"

"Certainly." Jo drew the slim holder from her back pocket and handed him a card. "I appreciate any business you send my way."

"Thanks." He beamed a bright smile at her, then walked down the drive. His well-fitting dark slacks accentuated his long legs. At the gate, he turned and gave her a brief wave.

Jo nibbled her bottom lip and followed the driveway to

the house. Interesting guy. A commanding physical presence, but he showed a lot of interest in the former renters. She halted. *Botheration.* She should have asked for his full name. The authorities might want to question him. Well, if he lived in the neighborhood as he claimed, they'd probably meet him.

Although he'd given his name as Gerald and not Boyd, Jo's senses were on full alert, and she hurried to the front door. The rhododendron shrubs ahead rustled. She sucked in a breath. The bottom leaves quivered the same dog she'd seen in the barn emerged. This time, a long piece of fabric, which looked vaguely familiar, dangled from his mouth. When he noticed Jo, he dropped the rag then scurried away.

"Come back, puppy dog. I won't hurt you." Still wary of the man she'd met, she hesitated to check on the dog's gift, but her conscience nagged at her. She had seen something similar recently.

Using a stick, she snagged a corner of the flimsy cloth, and held it up. Rosie's floral scarf. Jo reached out to touch the material, but stopped. Some of the pink and purple flowers had an ivory background, while others were surrounded by crimson...that seemed to be spreading. With the stick at arm's length, her gaze traveled down the fabric. Red droplets splattered onto the pavers. Blood? "Little dog, what have you done?"

A powerful motor purred behind Jo. She turned.

The Kitsap County Sheriff parked her forest-green SUV next to Jo's vehicle.

Carrying the bloody scarf on the stick, Jo approached the deputy. "I think the situation has changed."

Deceive Me Once:

Colors of Deceit:

Stolen Lives Trilogy:

Weep in the Night:

Day of Reckoning:

Justice at Dawn:

Forever Under Blue Skies:

Bio:

American Christian Fiction Writers Genesis Award winner Valerie Massey Goree resides in the beautiful Hill Country, northwest of San Antonio.

After serving as missionaries in her home country of Zimbabwe and raising two children, Valerie and her husband, Glenn, a native Texan, moved to Texas. She worked in the public school system for many years, focusing on students with special needs. Now retired, Valerie spends her time writing, traveling, and spoiling her grandchildren.

Novels include: *Deceive Me Once*; *Colors of Deceit*; The Stolen Lives Trilogy, *Weep in the Night*; *Day of Reckoning;* and *Justice at Dawn.* Valerie's latest novel, *Forever Under Blue Skies,* is set in Australia.

Valerie loves to hear from her readers.

Check Valerie's website to learn more about her romantic suspense novels and Glenn's non-fiction books: www.valeriegoreeauthor.com

Dear Reader:

Thank you for joining me on this journey to reveal the secrets Anna's mother kept for generations. I love research and since I'm not a scientist, I discovered a wealth of information about gene therapies. Most of the information I included is accurate, but given the license writing fiction provides, some of the details are, well, *fictitious*.

One caveat I need to stress. I refer back to a dark time in world history, in Germany specifically, as recorded in documents and testimonies. These events provide lessons from which we all can learn. I mean no disrespect to the country or the people.

I love connecting with my readers. Check out my Facebook author page. www.facebook.com/ValerieMasseyGoree   Or visit my website: www.valeriegoreeauthor.com
My books are also featured at: www.goodreads.com/search? and https://www.bookbub.com/search?

Sincerely,
Valerie Goree